Praise for *Here Be*

'*Here Be Leviathans* is a joy of a collection; one that's brimming with imagination and emotion. It'll make you laugh, think, and maybe even cry – sometimes all in the same story. A worthy successor to *Mammoth, Here Be Leviathans* highlights Chris Flynn as one of Australia's most unique and compelling writers.' ***The AU Review***

'The sheer audacity of Flynn's imagination is a bracing and liberating thing, and what could easily have turned into aimless whimsy is elevated by the author's bullseye wit. This hilarious, provocative collection effortlessly skewers human vice and folly.' ***The Sydney Morning Herald***

'In recent years, [Flynn] has begun to focus increasingly on the non-human. Humans people his new collection, too. They're just one of many characters. Not because humans are an afterthought, per se – rather, we are simply another species on a dying planet. Flynn is a restless experimenter, a fabulist. In the excellent final story, "Kiss Tomorrow Goodbye", his sinuous prose takes the reader through the underground tunnels of Las Vegas.' ***The Guardian***

'These stories are a broad palette, like looking at a Salvador Dali painting ... or [reading] Etgar Keret ... or Kurt Vonnegut – playful and wise. And the South American writer Borges as well ... your whole sense of how a story is told is bent out of shape. In the end they're about being human, and also about our lack of seniority in the environment and in the world – that the world matters as much as us.' ***The Bookshelf*, ABC Radio National**

Chris Flynn is the author of three novels, the most recent of which, *Mammoth*, was shortlisted for the Indie Book Awards and the Russell Prize for Humour. His work has appeared in *The Age*, *The Australian*, *The Guardian*, *McSweeney's*, *The Paris Review* and many other publications. He is Editor-in-Residence at Museums Victoria and the author of a series of picture books for children about Horridus, Melbourne Museum's *Triceratops*. Chris lives on Millowl (Phillip Island).

chriseflynn.com
@flythefalcon

Book club notes are available at www.uqp.com.au

HERE BE LEVIATHANS

CHRIS FLYNN

UQP

First published 2022 by University of Queensland Press
PO Box 6042, St Lucia, Queensland 4067 Australia
Reprinted 2022

University of Queensland Press (UQP) acknowledges the Traditional Owners and their custodianship of the lands on which UQP operates. We pay our respects to their Ancestors and their descendants, who continue cultural and spiritual connections to Country. We recognise their valuable contributions to Australian and global society.

uqp.com.au
reception@uqp.com.au

Cover design and illustration by WBYK
Illustrations by WBYK
Author photograph by Jo Duck
Typeset in 12/18 pt Sina Nova by Post Pre-press Group, Brisbane
Printed in Australia by McPherson's Printing Group

Queensland Government

University of Queensland Press is supported by the Queensland Government through Arts Queensland.

Australian Government | Australia Council for the Arts

University of Queensland Press is assisted by the Australian Government through the Australia Council, its arts funding and advisory body.

A catalogue record for this book is available from the National Library of Australia.

ISBN 978 0 7022 6277 7 (pbk)
ISBN 978 0 7022 6401 6 (epdf)
ISBN 978 0 7022 6402 3 (epub)

University of Queensland Press uses papers that are natural, renewable and recyclable products made from wood grown in well-managed forests and other controlled sources. The logging and manufacturing processes conform to the environmental regulations of the country of origin.

FSC www.fsc.org MIX Paper | Supporting responsible forestry FSC® C001695

Inheritance 1

22F 35

Monotreme 47

Here Be Leviathans 65

The Strait of Magellan 83

Alas, Poor Yorick 133

Shot Down in Flames 151

A Beautiful and Unexpected Turn 165

Kiss Tomorrow Goodbye 185

INHERITANCE

I ate a kid called Ash Tremblay yesterday. Parts of him, at least. The good bits. The crunchy skull, the brain, a juicy haunch. I was about to knuckle down to the messy business of stripping the skin from his back so I could feast on his organs when a ranger shot me in the face. It was Frances Locklear, of all the two-legs, from the National Park Service in Anchorage. I couldn't believe it.

I've always had a soft spot for Frances. She respected our kind. Kept a healthy distance. I ran into her once on the other side of the mountain, near Spencer Lake. She was fishing for trout and had earbuds in. Singing along merrily to what I now know was Depeche Mode's 'Enjoy the Silence'. Oh, the irony.

There's a story circulating among two-legs that if you play music or sing when you're out in the woods it deters bears. I mean, *maybe* if you're an especially bad singer or enjoy Coldplay at full volume, but it has the opposite effect on me. I'll come and say hello, see what you're up to. Besides, tinny speakers don't cut it. Someone should inform Samsung and Apple that their phones are not effective bear repellent. I scared the bejeesus out of two hikers last month when they finally noticed I was shadowing them from behind the bushes. I stalked them for over a mile before they fled in terror. I was only trying to listen to their music. Kendrick Lamar, I think. Not sure which album.

Anyway, there was Frances by the lake, oblivious. This will be funny, I thought. I'll amble up behind her and yawn, watch as she shits her pants. She didn't though. After the initial moment of shock and a glance at her out-of-reach-so-don't-even-think-about-it rifle, she tugged the buds from her ears, took a knee, bowed her head in deference to the fact her life was now entirely in my paws, and nodded towards the fish she'd caught, hoping I would eat them rather than her.

I was impressed. Plus, it seemed like a sweet deal, so that's what I did. A free breakfast is not to be sniffed at. I'll let you live this time, Frances, I thought. Go forth and tell your colleagues this unlikely tale. See how many of them believe you.

Have to say, I'm annoyed with her now. If I'd eaten her instead of those fish, this unfortunate incident could have been avoided. The bullet went through my lip and shattered a couple of teeth, which is bad news. It's early summer, and I have a ton of eating to do before the big sleep. It's going to be tough building up fat reserves if I can't chew properly. Frances might just have done me in. Still, I guess I was eating a teenager, and two-legs tend to frown upon our species indulging in such activities. If only he hadn't been so tasty.

Ingesting Ash's brain is causing me significant problems. Young Ash is the first two-legs I've devoured. Pops warned me about the risks, but I never really believed his stories. I seem to have absorbed the kid's memories and with them a surprising amount of knowledge about the two-legs' world. I know everything about this kid, all sixteen of his miserable years.

For example, last week in Girdwood, Ash was especially mean to his little brother, Cedar. He was idling behind a dumpster out the back of the Mercantile when Cedar and his friends rolled up on their bicycles. The boys didn't notice Ash as they dropped their bikes – he'd picked a solid spot for lurking.

I've not been into town since I was a curious youngster, but I've heard from Ralph One Ear and his crew of trash raiders that surprising treats can be gleaned from those dumpsters. They go at night, so the two-legs don't freak out at the sight of grizzlies rummaging through their leftovers. I'm much larger than Ralph though – too big to lumber through town, even under cover of darkness.

Ash watched as Cedar began locking his bicycle to the railing with a chain. This was met with hoots of derision from his friends Benny the Whistle and Shadonk-a-donk. Don't ask me what's going on with the names two-legs choose for their offspring these days.

'What're you locking that up for?' said Benny the Whistle. 'We'll only be in the Merc for five minutes, asshat.'

'So no-one steals it,' Cedar replied. 'Duh.'

'Who's gonna take your shitty bike?' Shadonk-a-donk asked. 'One of the dumb tourists?'

'You never know,' said Cedar, eyeing the group of middle-aged two-legs in bright puffer jackets who were waiting for the shuttle bus back to the resort.

'Leave it,' Benny the Whistle cautioned him. 'What if we have to make a quick getaway?'

Cedar wrapped the chain back around the saddle stem.

The boys slunk into the Mercantile to line their hoodie pockets with Jolly Ranchers or whatever junk pre-teens are fond of shoplifting. That was when Ash made his move. Emerging from his hiding place, he picked up his younger brother's bike and mounted it, popping wheelies as he waited for the kids to return.

When they did, the boys froze on the steps of the Mercantile even though their pockets were stuffed with stolen goods. This was merely the latest chapter in Ash's summer campaign of intimidation.

'Should've locked your bike, *asshat*,' Ash said. 'It's mine now.'

'Give it back,' Cedar ventured.

'Nah, I'm taking it for a ride,' Ash told him. 'See you dicks later.'

The young two-legs watched helplessly as Ash pedalled up the inclined street.

When Ash reached the highway, he stepped off the bike, wheeled it onto the bridge and, in one fluid movement, raised it above his head and threw it over the guard rail. The frame and wheels were swallowed by the roaring white water below.

I am the eldest in my family by ten minutes. I have two siblings: a brother and a sister. We used to get along quite well, back in the den. Those were good times. Mom would bring us pawfuls of huckleberries and, once, an entire deer. She showed us how to pick our teeth with its antlers, impressing upon us the importance of dental hygiene. When we were old enough, she took us to her favourite spot by the creek. It was packed full of fish, sluggish and flaking – freshwater salmon who'd swum out to sea then returned to spawn and die. They had adapted to the saltwater ocean and were rotting to death, unable to make it back to Turnagain Arm.

We feasted every night for weeks, gorging ourselves on eggs and eyes. I still visit that spot at the end of summer. It's easy pickings. Mom died a long time ago, but I always half expect to bump into my brother or sister at the creek. I haven't seen them in years. With the glaciers receding, more navigable territory has opened up. You can walk halfway to Canada if you time it right. My sister probably has cubs of her own now. I'd like to see them, my nieces and nephews, although a visit from the ornery old uncle may not be the wisest idea. Instinct might kick in. I'd probably eat them.

Pops wasn't around much after we were born for the same reason. Mom ran him off to ensure our safety. Once I was fully grown and had developed – and I'm being modest here – a reputation for ferocity around these parts, I sought my father out. I heard he was living over near Denali, which was one hell of a hike. But it was worth it. On a cold, clear night you can see the aurora. I would stand there for an age, staring up at the kaleidoscope of colours in the sky.

I found Pops living in a cave. He was old – almost thirty – and had fallen on lean times. His coat was dull and matted. He looked exhausted. Still charged out to challenge me, though. He was mighty relieved when I told him I was his son, and that I hadn't come to kill him.

We spent a couple of quality nights hunting together. Pops regaled me with wild tales of his travels, conquests, battles with moose and other critters, and of the time a couple of two-leg hunters pursued him for six cycles. Despite his bulk, Pops was a master of evasion. On the seventh night, he snuck around behind the hunters while they slept and slaughtered their horses. After that, it was only a matter of time before he prevailed. He had led them so far out into the wilderness that they would never make it back on foot.

The confrontation, when it came, was intense. Pops ambushed them so they didn't have time to unsling their rifles. He was on them before they could work out what was happening. The first two-legs reacted fast, all the same. He drew a pistol from a holster on his hip and shot Pops twice, but it was only a 9mm.

'What sort of amateur comes after a griz with a peashooter like that?' Pops asked me. 'I mean, come into my backyard with a .357 long barrel or don't come at all.'

With one swipe of his claw, the Glock – not to mention the arm holding it – flew in a graceful arc into the trees. The severed limb spattered an arterial blood trail on the first snows of winter. Then Pops chomped down on the two-leg's head and that was the end of him.

The second two-legs entered the fray at that point. Unable to get a shot off without hitting his partner, he charged right up to Pops and opened a canister of pepper spray.

'The stones on the guy!' Pops said. 'Though what else was he going to do, run? Good luck with that.'

This moron opened the can backwards and squirted it on himself instead of Pops. We're talking industrial-grade pepper spray here. The guy went down screaming. Pops watched him writhe around in the snow, blinded and in agony, while he gnawed on the first hunter's skull. Once Pops was done, he flipped the second guy over and carved open his back.

'You ate him even with that spicy shit on him?' I asked.

'Sure,' Pops said, licking his incisors at the memory. 'You leave it long enough, it's like seasoning.'

That was when he told me about inheritance of memory. After devouring the brains of those two-legs hunters, he knew all about their lives – their grim childhoods, their abusive fathers, their estranged families, their jobs in canning factories and on fishing boats, even their sexual proclivities.

'One rutted with females, whereas the other preferred males,' Pops told me. 'In fact, he was in love with his hunting partner, not that he'd ever mustered the courage to tell him.' He tapped the side of his huge head with a paw. 'They're together now, in here. Drives me nuts.'

I didn't really believe it at the time, although I'd heard rumours of similar stories – of bears living with two-legs, wolves and even a lynx in their head. It seemed fanciful, impossible even. Animals within other animals, memories layered on top of each other. The vanquished lingering in the minds of their conquerors. I figured the tales were exaggerated. Old bears are inveterate boasters. Still, Pops had access to an awful lot of information about those hunters and much of it seemed too specific for him to have made up. He was never that great a storyteller.

I enjoyed those weeks together. Sure, we disagreed, argued and fought – I still have the scars – but not many cubs get to have a relationship with their father, so I was lucky in that respect. I knew he wouldn't last many more winters. He'd get confused and wander off while in the middle of telling me something. When I'd call him back, he'd stare at me in fear for a few seconds, not recognising me.

'It's only me, Pops,' I'd say, and he'd relax, his hackles going down.

'I know,' he'd reply. 'I thought I saw something in the trees. A lynx, maybe, or an elk.'

'Could've been a sasquatch,' I would say, and he'd laugh.

'I've seen one, you know.'

'Here we go.'

A female with whom I had a brief dalliance three seasons later informed me that Pops was killed crossing the highway six months after I last saw him. The two-legs driving the truck had died too. Skidded off the road and slammed into the pines. Neither of them suffered. It was just – *bam*, lights out. The female apologised for being the harbinger of ill tidings. (Our kind prefer not to employ the term 'bearer of bad news'.) Our mating was successful. We had a litter of cubs together. I told them all about their grandfather's adventures so he wouldn't be forgotten. And then I left, as males do.

Ash's father left, too, shortly after Cedar was born, which goes some way to explaining the resentment Ash harboured towards his younger brother. That was when they lived back east, in Quebec. This memory inheritance lark has its advantages. I now have access to images of landscapes on the far side of the country, places I'll never have a chance to visit. The Tremblay family lived near a lake and Ash had a small boat. He'd row out onto the water when he was bored or depressed, which, given his miserable circumstances, was most of the time. He'd cast a line over the side and lie there for hours, listening to music and noodling himself. An awful lot of those memories. I had no idea two-legs masturbated so much. Try doing that with four-inch claws.

Sometimes, Ash would catch a fish. In his pent-up anger, he beat a few of them to death, but then he started to feel guilty about the senseless waste and brought them home for his mom to cook.

She was a good woman who'd had a hard life. She liked trees – hence the boys' unusual names – and red wine, and not much else. The most recent album she owned was from 1997 – Radiohead's *OK Computer.* Ash hated it. I haven't heard it myself. It's not the sort of thing hikers play in the woods.

His mother had worked the front desk in a car rental place in Quebec City, but, not long after her husband left, she moved to the opposite side of the continent, as far away from their problems as possible. Jobs were scarce in Anchorage, but she found employment sitting in a tollbooth at the entrance to Whittier Tunnel. The role was tedious and undemanding. Occasionally, she spotted a young bear charging across the highway. That would be the highlight of her week.

What Ash's mother didn't know is that every bear in the state is dying to run through that tunnel. It's the standard dare for wayward teens. No-one has ever done it, to my knowledge. The Whittier Tunnel is a two-and-a-half-mile shortcut under the mountain, but there's no way you're making it through on four legs without getting caught or hit by traffic. This does not stop us from congregating near the entrance. Two-legs call the area Bear Valley. Imagination has never been their strong point.

There's a woodland legend that Mackenzie Longclaw made it through the tunnel once by climbing on the back of a logging truck and hiding under a tarpaulin, but it sounds like guff to me. There's a bunch of Longclaw families scattered throughout the territory – it's a common surname – and they all claim Mackenzie was kin to them, yet no-one seems to have met him. The story raises some tricky questions, in my opinion. What did he do when the truck pulled in at Whittier? Leap down and treat himself to some reindeer sausage at the hot dog stand? Sneak onto a cruise ship? Don't mind me, everyone. Just a six-hundred-pound grizzly, here to check out the sights. Say, was that a beluga fin I just saw off the port bow?

While his mother tried to keep her feet warm in the tollbooth, Ash was left to his own devices. He turned his attention to the teenage population of Girdwood, none of whom were expecting a city kid with an axe to grind to be unleashed in their midst. Whatever property of theirs he liked, he kept. The rest he destroyed. He stomped toys and burst footballs. He slashed tires and tore clothing. He shoved and punched and kicked anyone who protested. When parents complained to his harried mother, Ash was nowhere to be found. When he turned up later and she attempted to reprimand him, he would tell her to shut the fuck up and skulk off to his room. In short, he was the most unhappy, disliked teenager in Girdwood, Alaska.

The only activity Ash truly enjoyed was running. Despite the dangers of potentially encountering one of my kind, he would set off in the early summer mornings up the mountain trail. Girdwood to the peak is only two miles, but it's an increase in elevation of two thousand feet. I've walked that trail myself and it's no joke. I was bushed by the end. Spectacular view, though. I was tempted to see if they would let me hitch a ride back down on the cable car but, alas, the weight limit is seven hundred pounds, and I weigh seven hundred and fifty.

Two-legs are always trying to prove how fit they are by embarking on ill-advised wilderness adventures. I've watched them climb rock faces and paddle rapids. Every time I think: what's the point? This tendency is especially irritating during the summer months. Two-legs come from far and wide to conquer the mountains, which is annoying when you're a local lad who has a limited window in which to build up fat reserves for the winter. Can't you do your extreme sports elsewhere?

That's how Ash Tremblay and I met. The Bird Ridge fun run. Although, I don't know what's fun about rushing through a predator-infested forest on a baking-hot day armed only with a bell. The kid could've been eaten by any one of the six bears in the area at the time. As it happens, he ran into me.

The glacial creek helps numb the pain in my snout. I hold my entire face under the freezing water for as long as I can, then I dip my paw in and wash the wound. We are daintier creatures than two-legs imagine. I can pluck the eyes from salmon; I can peel an egg. The creek runs pink, but the bleeding is slowing. Despite the throbbing soreness, I am still able to slurp some fluids into my dehydrated body. The left side of my tongue is shredded. Several teeth are now little more than sharp stumps. My gums are raw and bleeding. Fortunately, the bullet passed through my cheek and whizzed straight into the woods.

Frances must have shot me while I was turning to scarper. If I hadn't angled my head, the bullet would have wound up in my brain, and I would be dead. Frances is a good shot, and that M77 Hawkeye rifle of hers is loaded with .375 calibre Ruger cartridges. Pops would have admired her weapon and ammunition of choice. You'll get no arguments with that firepower, even from a behemoth like me.

I knew all about the Bird Ridge fun run. The event organisers had been crowing about it throughout the territory. There were posters everywhere and word got around on the critter grapevine. Basically, the message was: stay away from Bird Ridge and its environs. I tried to do exactly that, honest I did. But pre-hibernation mode is hard to ignore. I got peckish and went for a leisurely stroll to gather huckleberries. I was a model of savage innocence – I even went to great pains to learn the route from a flyer Ralph One Ear retrieved from a dumpster outside the resort. I was way off the beaten track, unlikely to bump into any red-faced two-legs huffing and puffing their way over the mountain, looking mighty foolish in lycra shorts with a number flapping on their chest.

Given my prudence, I was taken aback when Ash Tremblay burst forth from a thicket and skidded into my rump. My kind don't generally appreciate surprises. We tend to overreact.

Despite the boy's unwelcome intrusion on my berry-gathering jaunt, I still would have let him off with a warning, once I'd recovered from the shock collision. Bears don't really want to eat humans. If you happen to encounter one of us in the forest, remain calm. Sit down. Make yourself small. Maybe mutter a polite greeting. I know that's a bitter pill to swallow, but chances are if you stay cool, we'll sniff you and carry on with our business. That's exactly what happened when I was walking the ridgeline above California Creek last summer. I spotted two ATVs parked by the trees and moseyed on over for a look-see. It was a small tour group. The guide had led five two-legs down the slope to the creek below to pan for gold, but one feller had stayed behind to take photographs. He didn't hear me coming. I take after Pops when it comes to stealth.

I stopped beside him, sat on my haunches, and peered over the edge to see what he was photographing. He did the right thing. He made a funny little squeaking noise and froze. I sat next to him for a minute and only growled when I noticed he was slowly angling the camera towards me, presumably to get a selfie together. Look, it's an understandable instinct and I get why he did it. Proof. Maybe the final image of him alive and kicking. He quit when I made a low, guttural snarl. Started crying too. I felt sorry for the guy, so I ambled away into the woods, leaving him with piss in his pants and an unlikely story.

Most two-legged interlopers do one of two things upon encountering a grizzly. Neither is recommended. I don't know where people are sourcing their wilderness advice, but there must be some serious fake news out there.

Dumb response number one: make yourself as big as possible. Scream and holler. Roar. Let the animal know you're not to be messed with. Frighten them away. This requires some bravado, but the thing is, if you want to get into a scaring contest with me, there's only going to be one winner.

Dumb, albeit understandable, response number two: run.

I get why Ash took off down the trail. He was a runner. He'd been running his whole life, physically and metaphorically. The irony is not lost on me. He likely thought he could lick me in a foot race, since I outweighed him ten to one.

But he couldn't. You can't. Over a short sprint, I will take the pennant. We may be a sedentary species, but we are capable of great speed when necessary. And running away from a bear triggers an instinctual response that is virtually impossible to override. Running says, *I am prey*. No prizes for guessing what that makes me.

As I was charging Ash down, I had a few thoughts about the

situation. First, I'm hungry. Second, what is this kid doing so far off the official race route? He was taking a shortcut, wasn't he? What a cheater. Third, please do not tell me he's trying to take a photograph right now. What is with these two-legs and their phones?

Turns out he was only texting. Still extraordinary, given the circumstances. I read the exchange between mouthfuls of juicy flesh.

Ash sent Cedar the following message, an instant prior to three-quarters of a ton of angry beast landing on his back and snapping his spine: *Being chased by a bear, LOL!*

As last words go, I have to admit that was funny.

I was so caught up revelling in the gore and bloodlust that I was only vaguely aware of the phone ringing. Several texts pinged through as well. I paid them no heed. This was way better than huckleberries.

Stands to reason I'm a Luddite when it comes to technology. There was no way for me to know a rescue party was haring up the mountainside and that Ash's phone was leading them directly to my coordinates. It is truly astonishing what the two-legs have devoted their energies to these past few years. Didn't they once aspire to explore the stars? Cure epilepsy?

It was right around then that Frances Locklear shot me in the face, and I made good my escape. She's been hunting me for two days now. The time it took for the air ambulance to evacuate the remains of Ash Tremblay allowed me to build a good lead on Frances. This is not the first time two-legs have come after my hide, although admittedly Frances is the finest adversary I've faced thus far.

As I stand on the shore of the creek, I find the unparalleled beauty of my home moving. Low clouds pass over the face of the mountain and the permanent glacier pulsates blue. The air carries a thousand familiar scents. It will rain soon.

I think of Cedar. I imagine him trudging around Girdwood with a backpack full of stolen property. Now his brother is gone, it has fallen on him to return the items to their rightful owners. With each door he knocks, he faces insincere consolation, the guilt of relief. No-one misses Ash Tremblay, not even his brother or his mother, not really. Some in the community are probably glad he's dead. If someone had to be taken, Ash was the one they would gladly have sacrificed. They won't say that aloud, of course. They will offer words of solace, platitudes. Sorry for your loss. Our thoughts and prayers, et cetera. They will wait for my head to be triumphantly presented to the Tremblay matriarch. *Here is the rogue grizzly that took your son*, the hunters will proclaim. *Justice has been served. Vengeance is thine.*

They'll have to catch me first. I have a new weapon in my arsenal they don't know about: Ash's memories. I know all about the two-legs now. Their habits. Their fears. Their wickedness.

I find shelter in a nearby den that's marked with many scents. I detect pungent fox, astringent wolf and a faint, vaguely comforting smell. It takes me a moment, but eventually I work out that it is the scent of Cyclops George. He and I had a few run-ins a couple of years back. It was a territory thing. I won, obviously. George had his left eye gouged out by a branch while fleeing. I felt bad about that, but he got his fair share of licks on me too. Bit me in the hindquarters. Not very sporting. I couldn't sit down properly for a fortnight. I think he headed east over the glacier to the great forest beyond.

He never came back this way. If he could see the mess I'm in now, he'd be licking his chops at the prospect of usurping me as alpha.

It's good to find a cosy den. My days are usually spent lumbering around the mountain, grazing and contemplating the majesty of nature. Us bears are normally only active in short bursts. This relentless pursuit business has me spent. I could sleep for a week except I need to keep going, to penetrate so deep into the wilderness that Frances Locklear will never find me.

Ash Tremblay comes to me with sleep. It's a dream, I guess, though it may also be infection-induced delirium. I can't really tell. There he is, sitting on the steps of the Mercantile, watching me as I sniff around the dumpsters, hunting for ripe leftovers.

'I had ambitions, you know,' Ash says.

'You're blaming me for curtailing your aspirations of athletic glory?' I ask, as I overturn a garbage pail full of lettuce.

'I could've gone to the Olympics,' he says. 'At the very least, the Commonwealth Games. I wanted to compete for Canada.'

'Need I remind you that when our fateful meeting occurred you were cheating?'

'I would've got away with it too,' Ash says, scowling. 'My plan was to shave a mile off the course and pop out before the next checkpoint. Those dumbass stewards wouldn't have known a thing.'

'What about karma?' I ask him. 'Maybe you got what you deserved.'

'My face eaten off for taking a shortcut on a fun run? That's harsh, bro. The punishment doesn't fit the crime.'

'It's what our kind call natural justice,' I tell him.

'You should be the one concerned about karma.'

'How so?' I ask, raising my snout from rummaging.

'Because I'm in here with you, asshat,' Ash says. 'I'm in your head, in your dreams. You killed me, and now I'm going to mess you up big-time.'

'If this is a dream, then I can do whatever I want,' I tell him. 'Right now, I'm tempted to kill you all over again.'

'If you want to scavenge for scraps, we should walk down to the Double Musky Inn,' he says, ignoring the empty threat. 'They might have rotting salmon heads in their dumpster.'

'Rotting salmon is still salmon.'

Apart from Ash, the town of Girdwood is bereft of citizens. The rear doors of a mail truck flap open outside the post office. Clothing is strewn on the ground outside the second-hand store, Thriftwood. The vinyl banner over the laundromat has come away from its moorings and droops onto the deck below. It reads: *The World-Renown Girdwood Laundromall, Voted America's #1 Laundromat.* In addition to laundry (self and drop-off), the establishment offers showers, wi-fi, an ATM, cannabis, Thai food, a hair salon, massage and an art gallery.

'Those amenities dovetail nicely,' I say to Ash as we walk past.

'Smoking weed's not as much fun when it's legal.' Ash thrusts his hands deep into his pockets. 'Their Massaman curry wasn't bad though.'

'I've not had the pleasure.' I tentatively sniff the air.

'I hope I tasted good, at least.'

'You're no caribou. Still pretty succulent. Harder to catch, but the chase was worth it.'

'Aren't caribou fast?' Ash asks.

'Yes, but they're dumb as all get-out. They'll keep grazing the tundra right up to the moment you land on their neck. Fortunately, there's plenty of them. Good breeders.'

'That wound on your mouth looks nasty,' Ash says. 'You want to get that looked at before it turns septic.'

'Your concern is touching.'

'I don't want you to die, not that easily. Especially now I get to torture you psychologically.'

'I'll get over it,' I tell him.

As we wander down to the Double Musky Inn parking lot, the emptiness of the place strikes me as odd. Ash perches on the deck, ruefully peering at the pool table inside. I pause in my refuse scavenging to take in the surroundings of Girdwood. The sun is low in the sky. It will rain in about an hour. I hear no birdsong in the woods. It could be a quiet Sunday morning, out of tourist season.

'My dreams are not usually this lucid,' I say.

Ash scoffs. 'Who said you were dreaming?'

'What else could it be?'

'We'll talk more soon,' Ash tells me.

'Are you going somewhere?' I ask him, as he stands up and brushes down his jeans.

'No, but you are,' he says. 'Can't you smell that?'

I raise my snout to the wind. An alarming scent wafts through my nostrils. The smell is distant, yet familiar. The faint sweat of a two-legs, carried on the breeze.

Ash laughs at my confusion. 'Better wake up, murderer.'

I emerge from feverish sleep with a jolt. I lift my head and look around, disoriented, my breathing laboured. I am in a den.

Cyclops George once hibernated here. It is shallow. Not safe. The light of dawn filters through the undergrowth. I sniff the morning air.

There it is again. That distinctive scent. I'd know it anywhere, ever since that day by Spencer Lake. Frances Locklear. She is hiking up the valley towards me. She's been walking all night, by the smell of her. That takes dedication. Determination. Admirable qualities if she weren't intending on putting a bullet in my brain. I am impressed. I knew she was good, but I didn't expect this. Perhaps she knows the Tremblay family and feels obliged to hunt me down out of solemn duty. Maybe there's a price on my head.

Whatever the reason, she is almost here. I rouse myself and search for scent markers. Two-legs are easy to track unless they know how to camouflage their odour. Some of them do. The real clever hunters. They smear themselves with the excrement of a young moose and hide in the bushes until one of us comes around investigating potential dinner. Next thing you know, your head's mounted on some rich guy's wall after he blows off your hindquarters with an RPG. I'm not kidding. The open carry laws in Alaska mean two-legs could walk into the Double Musky Inn with a Patriot missile under each arm.

Frances would never be so unsporting, but if she's hiked through the woods at night to try and catch up to me, then she surely means business.

I emerge from the den and stretch. I am hungry, but that's always the case. My jaw aches. My gums throb. I roll my tongue over sharp tooth stumps to remind myself that it was Frances who caused this pain. She shot me and will do so again if she gets the chance.

A light mist floats over the tree line below. I am in an elevated position, with a clear view of the forest. I hear Frances now, trudging through the woods, cursing under her breath. She sounds exhausted. Just about ready to throw in the towel and turn back. Her smell sharpens as she emerges from cover a mile below. She is a wraith, tired and grim. She takes off her hat and runs a hand through her short hair, then surveys the landscape, glad to be out of the dense woodland. It's slippery in there. A two-legs could easily turn an ankle.

Frances removes a map from the pouch on her jacket. She crouches to spread it out on her knee and get her bearings. I stand perfectly still, waiting for her to spot me. Her eyes scan the hillside and pass over my body. She doesn't see me at first. It occurs to me that I blend in with the background, so I tilt my head. An almost imperceptible movement, but I want to test how good she is.

She does a double-take. I turn my snout, curl back my lip and raise a paw to point at the wound she caused, so there can be no mistake that I am the one she seeks.

Frances slowly folds the map and puts it away, then unslings her M77 Hawkeye rifle. That will do the job, alright, but she must perform under difficult circumstances. The elevation, a stiffening breeze, the fact she is a little over a mile away and fatigued – good luck hitting me in those conditions.

I stand my ground and let her take the shot. With a bit of luck, she will spare me the fate of expiring in fevered agony from infection. I take in the wilderness around me in case these are my final moments.

Frances raises the rifle and adjusts the scope. Shakes out her shoulders. Sucks in a few deep gulps of cold air and then exhales.

Her breath billows out in a plume of white. She steadies the rifle against her shoulder and pulls the trigger.

I know I am not shot because the .375 calibre bullet whizzes past so close that my left ear twitches. Nice try, Frances. You almost had me. Those crosswinds are tricky to predict.

I decide to try faking her out. If she underestimates me, I may gain an advantage. I roar in pain, acting like I've been mortally wounded. Frances pumps the air with her fist, congratulating herself on her marksmanship. I bet she can't wait to tell the rangers in Anchorage about that incredible shot. She pulls back the bolt so the empty cartridge pops out, and slams it forward to chamber another round. Then she stands up and hustles forward onto the shale. She intends on tracking the blood trail until she can get in close and finish me off.

Frances eagerly scrambles up the slope. It is not easy going. The scree is loose, and she struggles to find purchase.

She slips, falls on her face and tumbles back down to where she started. She is shaken but unhurt, other than a few cuts and bruises. She checks her rifle for damage and evinces relief. Lucky. If the barrel of that M77 had bent she'd be screwed.

I shake my head and issue a challenging roar, all fangs and slobber. It hurts my jaw, but it's worth it to see the look on Frances's face. She takes a step back and blinks, slumping to her knees in the loose shale. She is wondering if I am worth the effort. It's a fair question. I shall leave you to reflect on that, Frances Locklear. Rest up and ponder whether you want to die out here in the wilderness, torn limb from limb. While you're doing that, I'll be somewhere over the next hill, waiting for you to catch up.

—

Another stream offers welcome respite. I drink deeply, aware that I might not have the opportunity to do so again for a while. Then I sit on my hindquarters to rest and strategise. If I hurried, I could double back around Bird Ridge and ambush Frances from behind, or at least cut her off and force her further into the ranges. The longer she stays out, the more haggard she will become.

But I eschew this plan. It's impossible for me to walk anywhere around here and not leave a trail. Frances won't be so easily fooled. If she keeps up the pursuit, she will be cautious. She knows I'm dangerous. No-one ever tried to keep a grizzly as a pet. Well, no-one in their right mind, at any rate. I wonder if Frances has a similar reputation. Is she considered reckless? A risk taker? Someone not to be wronged?

Then I realise I know a lot more about her than I did two days ago. I have access to an entirely new set of memories about this ranger from Anchorage.

Ash didn't like Frances much. He met her when she came to his school in Girdwood to give a talk on animal rights and respecting nature. It did not go down well with Ash, who was, at that time, actively engaged in trapping and torturing whichever furred creatures he could get his grubby fourteen-year-old hands on. That's an alarm bell, right there. Future serial killer in the making. I'm glad I ate him. Probably saved a bunch of female two-legs from winding up in his cellar, chained to a boiler.

'We don't own this land,' Frances told the assembled students. 'That's an illusion. The territory is a vast, living entity. If anything, the land owns us. We elevate ourselves above nature, assume that we are lords of the natural world, when, really, we are one single element of the ecosystem, and an aggressive one at that. We need to forge a more integral, holistic approach with the animal kingdom, which would be healthier for all parties. The desire for ownership is toxic. Conquest, disenfranchisement, slavery, the wholesale slaughter of animals, intolerance – none of these have been good for us as a species.'

'Yeah, whatever,' Ash interrupted, to the horror of his teacher, Mr Borland (whom he called Mr Bored-land).

'That's enough, Ash,' Mr Bored-land said.

'It's alright,' Frances assured him, then addressed Ash directly. 'You don't agree?'

'Fuck, no,' Ash said.

Mr Bored-land threw his hands in the air.

Ash shifted in his chair and corrected himself. 'I mean, no, I don't. Humans conquered nature. We beat it. We won. We have the right to chop everything down and eat anything that moves. The land's not alive. We are. It's there to sustain us.'

'Sustain being the operative word,' Frances said. 'What happens once we've exhausted all the resources?'

'Find another planet. Use this one as a garbage dump.'

'You're being unnecessarily provocative, Ash,' Mr Bored-land said.

'I'm just providing an alternative to this hippy tree-hugging bullshit.'

'Alright, that's enough,' Mr Bored-land said. 'Report to the principal's office, Ash. I'll not have you insult our guest.'

'Weren't you named after a tree?' Frances said, opening her arms. 'Does that mean I can hug you, Ash? Come on, bring it in.'

The students laughed.

Ash muttered under his breath as he shoved books into his bag.

'One more word and you're suspended,' Mr Bored-land said.

Ash shot daggers at Frances as he passed her on the way to the door. His memory of Frances ends there.

The long, buzzy tone of a varied thrush nearby draws me back to the mountainside. I should follow her. She might lead me to a red huckleberry bush. My mother once told me that the bark could act as a salve against toothache. I will find a shrub and strip its leaves, then pack bark into my mouth. These broken stumps are excruciatingly painful, and I fear they will plunge me into a foul mood for weeks. While they throb, I will not be able to sleep. I am in dire need of modern dentistry.

That night, I smell rabbit. Dead rabbit, cooking over an open fire. It is not an animal I have eaten often. Too fast for me to catch, and not much of a meal anyway.

A convenient southerly breeze kept me informed regarding the location of my stalker all day. Dispirited and tired, Frances made slow progress until eventually she gave up and camped in a clearing I passed through around midday. She's been there ever since. I am unsure if this means she has abandoned the chase or is merely recovering her energy to renew the pursuit tomorrow. Either way, it is time to go on the offensive and settle this, once and for all. Also, that rabbit smells delicious, so events are, to a degree, being dictated by my stomach, which got me into this pickle in the first place.

I do not need to mask my presence as much by night. There

are numerous nocturnal animals conducting their business in the forest. The sun did not dip behind the mountains until late in the evening and will rise early, so there are only a few hours available in which to gather food, procreate and catch up on woodland gossip. As I make my way back along the trail towards the ranger's encampment, a boreal owl winnows from a branch overhead. I pause for a moment to watch as she rotates her head, seeking insects, voles or a potential mate. What a skill, to be able to look behind you like that. I can barely see my own hind legs.

By the time I reach Frances's camp, it is darkest night. The moon is a waning sliver, and the main source of light is the glowing campfire. I quietly observe the scene from behind a Northern Gold shrub. Flames still dance in the firepit. Frances made it large, presumably to deter predators. An entire cooked rabbit is skewered on a stick protruding from the earth. Frances's sleeping bag is rolled out on the ground, under a birch. I can smell her, curled up inside. No sign of the rifle. I guess she's sleeping with it. I will have to be careful but, still, this is a shame. Too easy. I almost feel bad.

In as much as it is possible for me to do so, I tiptoe across the clearing, fighting the urge to stop by the fire and snack on that rabbit. It only takes a moment to reach the sleeping bag. I place my paws carefully on the earth, so as not to step on any fallen branches and alert the dozing ranger. Poor Frances. She must have been really beat. It was a good effort. I'll give her that.

She is really snuggled in there. I hook a claw into the zipper ring and draw it down. As I am doing so, Ash is in my mind, tutting and shaking his head. *The rabbit*, he says. *Think about the rabbit, asshat.*

Odd that an experienced ranger like Frances would roast an

entire rabbit and stake it to the ground by the fire. Why would she cook something she had no intention of eating? Surely the heady odour would only draw hungry critters to her camp.

I open the sleeping bag. Inside is Frances's backpack. I detect an exhalation of breath from the branches of the birch above and throw my bulk against the trunk just as the crack of a rifle shot shatters the peaceful night.

The bullet grazes my right thigh, tearing a painful streak in the flesh. If I had not moved so fast, I would be already dead. Knowing Frances must reload, I repeatedly pound the tree, roaring.

It is a not a particularly robust specimen and the trunk fractures, causing the upper branches to dip towards the ground. Frances falls out and lands awkwardly on her face. The strap of the M77 catches around a branch, tugging the rifle from her grasp.

I stand upright on my hind legs, ready for the kill but curious to see what she does next.

Rising to a crouch, Frances draws a knife from the scabbard on her belt. She kicks one foot back, poised for attack. I have seen an expression like hers before, on animals who know they are about to die but who are determined to go down fighting. It is better this way. Honourable. And brave. That's a word that gets bandied about too often these days, but Frances Locklear staring down a seven-hundred-and-fifty-pound injured grizzly, armed only with a knife? Gold standard.

The first inkling of an alternative outcome stirs in my brain, or should I say *our* brain. To my surprise, I find myself standing down. I regard Frances, all fear and fury, backlit by flames, and decide to try something.

I extend a single claw, point it at her, then indicate the bloody mess on my snout and give her a look as if to say, *'See what you did? You get that I'm pissed, right?'*

This, understandably, gives the two-legs pause. Her brow furrows. The knife wavers.

Sign language is not my specialty, but I muddle through. I point at the rabbit, then my mouth.

Frances grunts, her face a model of concern. Stoicism worked for her once before. After a moment's hesitation, she waves me towards the rabbit. I nod gratefully, slide the meat from the skewer with the utmost care and pop it into my welcoming maw. Despite being cooked, it is surprisingly tasty. I try to convey this with a *'Hey, that's not bad'* expression.

Frances slides warily out of her fighting stance.

I press forward with communication. This is a first, for both our species. Neither of us is especially qualified as a linguistic pioneer. I point to my chest and then the looming mountains. Next, I point at Frances and suggest she proceed in the opposite direction.

Frances blinks repeatedly. She is trying to process this startling development. 'You want to go our separate ways?' she asks.

I nod.

She exhales. When she speaks again, I detect a quiver of emotion in her voice. 'Fuck me,' she says. 'You understand what I'm saying?'

I shrug.

'I don't ... I can't ... how is this possible?' she says.

Where does one even begin when trying to explain such a phenomenon? If only I had the power of two-legs' speech. Alas, I fear my larynx is not suited to their awkward vowels. I shrug again.

'O ... kay,' she says, sliding the knife back into its sheath.

'I don't know what's going on here, but I'm guessing we're calling a truce. Am I reading that right?'

I sigh with relief and nod assent. I don't want to kill her. I have enough problems as it is.

'This isn't a trick?' she asks.

I trace a claw across my chest in the shape of a cross and plonk myself down by the fire. Wide-eyed, Frances sits on a log beside me.

'I'm supposed to kill you for eating that kid,' she says, after a while. 'I guess that's off the cards now. I don't suppose you'd consider coming back to town with me? We could try to explain all this.'

I give her a weary look.

'Probably not a good idea,' she says, gnawing her lip. She is surprisingly calm, all things considered, although the thousand-yard stare in her eyes tells the story of someone who has passed beyond the realms of accepted dogma and is beginning to understand that her comprehension of the world up to this point has been severely limited.

'I really messed up your mouth, didn't I?' she says.

I raise my bloody lip to display her handiwork.

She grimaces. 'Sorry about that. I didn't know.'

You and me both, lady.

We sit in silence for a while. Frances is rather lost for words. But the day is catching up to me. I am faltering.

'Will you be alright out there?' she asks, looking up at the mountains.

I shake my head. No, Frances Locklear, I will not. But let us spend one peaceful night together. The fire is warm and pleasant. The tension that has been present in my limbs since the incident on Bird Ridge seeps out into the earth and disperses. I am no longer hunted. My wounds ache but I have warm food in my belly. Not much, but enough to stave off hunger. Yes, it is possible Frances might betray my trust and kill me while I slumber, but wouldn't that be a tender mercy? I would rather it be her than some cowardly hunter seeking a trophy. Frances would approach my death with reverence and sorrow.

The life of a grizzly is one of isolation and loneliness. We are resented, feared and spurned. How astonishing that I can communicate, however rudimentarily, with a two-legs, our great adversary. What wonders might our species achieve together if further discussion were possible? We could redefine compassion and see the world anew. We could find grace. If only I could live.

I stand next to a crisp, clear lake. The sun dips behind unfamiliar hills and the fading light casts purple shadows across the stilled surface of the water. Tiny birds flit back and forth, hunting insects. As darkness approaches, it is easier to follow their reflections than their actual flight. They speak to each other in bursts of squeaky chatter.

'What are they?' I ask Ash, who is crouching and skipping flat stones across the face of the water.

'Wrens,' he tells me. 'Mom found a nest in her clothes-pin bag once. We had to wait until the eggs hatched and the chicks flew away before we could hang anything on that section of line.'

'Is this where you grew up?' I ask him.

The boy nods solemnly. 'Just after Dad took off.'

'We have travelled back in time,' I say. 'We can do that?'

'I guess. That's what memories are, right?'

'I like it here,' I tell him, dipping a paw in the cold water.

'We never heard from him again,' Ash says, standing and kicking in the shallows. 'Can you believe that? What kind of douche-nozzle leaves his wife and two sons and then never contacts them? Not a single card or an email or a fucking Facebook friend request. I don't even know if he's still alive.'

'Such is the male nature,' I tell him. 'I left my cubs too.'

'Yeah, but if you'd stayed, you'd have eaten them. It's hardly the same.'

'True.' I look at the cabin set back from the lake. Smoke plumes lazily from the chimney. It smells of thorn. 'Well, it's unorthodox,' I say, 'but for what it's worth, I'm here now. We are one, Ash.'

The boy scrunches up his face. He thinks on this for a moment before inhaling deeply. He seems resigned to his fate now. Our fate.

'Suppose.' He shrugs. 'Fucking grizzly stepdad. Didn't see that coming.'

'It won't be for much longer.'

'You're going to die, aren't you?' Ash says. The boy is sharper than he looks.

'What are the chances Frances Locklear shoots me while I sleep?' I ask him.

'Zero,' Ash says, snorting. 'Not her style. She'll be racked with guilt at the thought of hurting you in the first place.' He waves a hand dismissively. 'Nah, she'll be gone in the morning. Scuttled back to the ranger station in Anchorage with a made-up story, trying her best to forget what happened. Why'd you have to give the game away with your embarrassing attempts at sign language?'

'I didn't want to kill her,' I say. 'Did you really want her in here with us?'

'Fuck, no,' Ash says.

A breeze ruffles my fur. Ripples form where a fish rises to pluck a fly skating across the surface of the water.

'I am going to die, and soon. My jaw is ruined. But I am carrying reserves. It will take weeks for me to starve. Perhaps months. I will lose my mind. The smell of salmon in the river will render me insane. That will not be pleasant for either of us, Ash.'

'We could kill ourselves,' Ash says. 'Can bears do that?'

'In theory, yes. I could cast myself into a gorge. It would be contrary to instinct, though. I'm not one hundred per cent certain I could go through with it.'

'Turn back towards Girdwood, then,' Ash says. 'Go down in a hail of bullets.'

'That would be glorious,' I say, imagining my final charge. 'But it would give the two-legs satisfaction, not to mention lurid bar stories. And it would reinforce the stereotype of a crazed grizzly bearing down on its hapless victims. Nature red in tooth and claw. Not good for the reputation of my kind.'

'Why do I get the impression there's a suggestion coming?' Ash says.

'Already, we know each other too well,' I say, strolling through the pellucid water to stand next to the two-legs teenager. Something blooms in my chest. I feel protective of this boy. A sense of ownership. No, not quite that. Paternalism, borne from guilt at his abandonment, at my own. I want him to live forever.

'Your whole life, you felt alone,' I say.

'More a loner than alone.'

'There is a way we can stay together, you and I,' I tell him. 'We can run free through the mountains and breathe freezing air.

Our paws will take us places no two-legs have ever been. Would you like that, Ash?'

The boy looks between the cabin and the lake. This is his past. He does not want to be stuck here. I can offer him a future, the likes of which no human has experienced.

'Fuck it,' he says, laughing and rolling his eyes. 'I'm in, *Dad*.'

'Call me Pops.'

When we awaken by the crumbling embers of the fire and Frances Locklear is gone, we will eat the extra rabbit she left behind for us. Then, revived, we will head north, deeper into the mountains. A pack of wolves live up near Knik River. Every winter, they're a pain in the rump. They terrorise the forest, eating all our small four-legged friends and disturbing every sleeping bear in the neighbourhood with their constant howling and carrying on.

We will take them on and see how many we can kill before we succumb. A minor act of community service. In years to come, the denizens of the glacier will commemorate the day. Remember the bear exile from Bird Ridge who ate that teenage two-legs, they'll say. He messed up those wolves. It took a dozen of them to bring him down.

The wolves will talk about us in their dens on cold nights. Tell their pups how Ash Tremblay and I fought for hours. How our flesh sustained the pack during a rough winter. How we run with them now.

Those wolves will never forget us. They won't be able to. They will inherit our memories.

22F

The first day in a new workplace is always nerve-racking. So many new faces. A bewildering stream of introductions. The establishment of hierarchy. Who will I like? Who are the snipers, the gossips to avoid? Which boss is friendly and which one's a sleaze? Who will gladly help if you're unsure about an unfamiliar IT system? Where are the bathrooms?

Where they always are, of course. Situated at the rear of the aircraft, in the midsection over the wing and at the back of business class. Smoking is not permitted at any time. Detectors have been installed. Should the seatbelt sign be illuminated, please return to whichever of us you were allocated.

Personalities become apparent within the first week. There are the jokers, always primed for a quip or sarcastic comment about a passenger. 19B and 16D are the worst. They never let up. It's a constant battle of one-upmanship to see who can tell the most outrageous story. They go too far sometimes, leaching the humour out of the situation. Then there are the depressives who hate their jobs and constantly complain about matters beyond our control. Delays, spillages, rowdy children. At first, I lent a sympathetic ear, but you can only listen to someone gripe about the same old things for so long before you start avoiding them. I wish 20C could hear themselves sometimes. You would think they had the worst life imaginable.

Then you have the stirrers. There are a few of those, but 25A is the one to watch. They're always monitoring conversations, listening for something to use against you. Even the most innocuous of comments is exaggerated out of proportion. You say something glib and offhand, and next thing you know you're being accused of bullying or confronted by one of your co-workers about something you allegedly said. It's such a shame we have seats like that. It creates an unnecessary tension in the workplace. Hopefully, they'll be replaced in a refit but there is probably precious little chance of that. They'll be grinning till the bitter end, all the while twisting a knife in your tray table.

I am a hardworking but unremarkable employee and perform my job without complaint and without expecting plaudits. That's what most of us are, in truth. The comedians, the whingers and the toadies are exceptions to the rule. And yet I suppose it would be a less colourful workplace without them.

Passengers are a different breed entirely. I've had all sorts. Overweight, underweight, adults, children, winners, losers, priests, thieves, actors, doctors, students, teachers, somebodies and nobodies. I have eavesdropped on a thousand boring conversations where one party would have done virtually anything to be moved to another seat. I have also borne witness to excited meetings between strangers who left the aircraft with the intention of becoming more intimately acquainted. Sometimes they can't wait that long, and they sneak into one of the bathrooms for an illicit tryst. We hear all about it later. No salacious detail is spared. I try not to pay attention. Toilets are inveterate boasters and disgusting perverts. You can't believe half of what they say.

For the most part, passengers eat and sleep and squirm and break wind. They listen to music, watch movies and yearn for it all to be over. When we land, they cannot wait to stand up and take their bags from the overhead lockers. Even if they won't disembark for another ten minutes, they still lurk gormlessly in the aisles, as if the ground crew might have somehow worked out how to speed up the process this time around.

It doesn't take long to settle into a routine and no longer register passengers' faces. You stop caring. You simply want the working day to be over.

Occasionally, something memorable happens. A man had a heart attack and died in 18E. They won't forget him in a hurry. He spent the final few hours of that flight covered with a blanket while a stranger slept next to him, oblivious. 12D had their upholstery replaced after a pregnant woman's waters broke all over them. The child was born on the aircraft, behind a privacy curtain in business. Pretty much the only way to get an upgrade these days.

15A and 15B were embroiled in an incident where two passengers fornicated under a blanket. This happens more often than you might think and is rarely noticed by the flight attendants. In that case, it was blatant. The couple was arrested upon arrival at our destination. If only they had been more discreet, like the multitudes who pleasure themselves under the cover of darkness.

The nervous passengers are the worst. The fretters, the anxiety-ridden, the vomiters. Those who are convinced we will plummet from the sky because an engine will fall off, or that we will be struck by lightning, or have a mid-air collision, or be overrun by terrorists. I have observed conspiracy theorists cast their steely glare around the aircraft until they spot a likely suspect. A man with a long beard, perhaps. Nothing ever happens, but they are always primed to be the hero, to wrestle the perceived terrorist to the floor and defuse the bomb by cutting the green wire, just like they saw in the inflight entertainment.

Something truly memorable did happen to me, eventually. Not a birth or a bolt of lightning, but the event that defined who I am now.

This is the story of my final day at work.

The start of the flight was unremarkable. We took off on schedule. We crossed desert and ocean and islands. We travelled back in time. My passenger was a young woman, accompanied by her mother in my colleague 22E. They were a quiet seat, content with their lot. Not a huge personality. Not a thinker, like me. We often passed our time in silence.

The young woman was taking her mother on holiday. They planned to disembark at our refuelling stop and catch a connecting flight to their final destination.

The mother spoke in hushed Cantonese. Her daughter replied in English with elongated Australian vowels. She said things like, 'Settle down, Mum,' and called her a 'dag'.

They removed their shoes. The mother had brought her own eye mask and neck-support pillow. In her small carry-on backpack, the daughter had a book, a Ziploc® bag of trail mix, a spare pair of underwear, a packet of mints, her wallet, house keys, her passport and half-a-dozen *My Favorite Murder* podcast episodes downloaded onto her phone. She was set up for a flight without much interaction with her mother, perhaps expecting the older woman to sleep for most of it.

The incident occurred over Kamchatka. You hear about such things but never expect it to happen to you. The aircraft shook and bucked. Warning lights flashed. Oxygen masks dropped. Unsecured passengers fell from us. Even those wearing seatbelts were thrown violently forward, many unable to raise their arms in time to prevent striking their heads on the tray tables in front. Everyone screamed and shouted and prayed. The aircraft banked sharply, dropping hundreds of feet in seconds. I understood the end was nigh when a crack snaked up the cabin wall towards my window.

Was it a bomb? I don't think so. The explosion would have come from within. No, something hit us. Not another aircraft or a flock of geese but an object – something sleek and powerful struck the fuselage with destructive force.

The passengers really panicked when the crack zigzagged across the ceiling directly over my row. Several unfastened their seatbelts and attempted to clamber over the injured and stunned, charging towards the front in the false belief they might find a haven in business class, or at least nicer biscuits.

The young woman helped place an oxygen mask over her mother's face before attaching her own, contrary to guidelines. She gripped her mother's arm and they shut their eyes. There was no way to say goodbye over the noise. I held her tightly in preparation for what was to come.

With a wrenching sound, the crack widened and air rushed in – freezing air that snatched the breath of anyone not wearing a mask. The aircraft's nose dipped. Carry-on baggage and loose passengers tumbled past my row and slammed into the bulkhead near the bathrooms. The crack gaped and then the tail section sheared off. Rows 23 and beyond vanished.

The young woman strained to look behind as the tail spiralled away into a backdrop of stars. People fell from their seats into the void. There was no fire, merely a separation. Our section began to spin. An attendant and a beverage trolley whizzed past and were sucked out. Then a shuddering commenced at my base.

Our row was breaking free from its moorings. The carpet tore. Bolts pinged. The young woman cried out in pain. Then, a suck of air, and we were no longer inside the aircraft.

This was a new experience for me, being outside. Cold air buffeted my upholstery. I was flying, truly flying, without any assistance. We spun around and the young woman and her mother screamed, but their cries were smothered by the rushing wind. The front section of the aircraft hurtled past, blue flame licking the underside of the fuselage. Seats and bags and people tumbled from the gaping hole.

Rows 21 and 20 followed us out. That'll finally give 20C something legitimate to complain about.

The front section was several hundred feet below us when it exploded in a burst of orange. Debris was blown towards us and a jagged piece of metal impaled the old woman in 22E, slicing through her belly and severing the seatbelt. The young woman attempted to hold on to her mother, but she was ripped away.

We were alone now, she and I. My quiet friend 22E had been

virtually destroyed, their remains hanging loose, their insides splayed open. The young woman screamed for a moment longer, then passed into unconsciousness. We fell the rest of the way in silence.

The Sea of Okhotsk stretched out to the south. As we spiralled down, I made out the Kamchatka Peninsula below, a remote and largely uninhabited place. We would not sink into the ocean's watery depths. I would experience one final landing.

It took a minute for us to make landfall. The young woman did not regain consciousness. That was for the best. Although my belt held her in place, her limbs and neck were broken by the velocity at which we hit the canopy. She was already lifeless when my row struck the earth and became embedded in the dank soil of the Siberian forest.

What remained of 22E was thrust deep into the ground. Most of me still protruded. The body of the young woman prevented me from being forced too far under the hard-packed dirt.

I do not know what happened to the rest of the aircraft and my colleagues. Perhaps they sank into the Sea of Okhotsk. Perhaps they were scattered over kilometres of remote mountainous terrain. None of them landed anywhere near us.

Rain fell that first night. Although I had seen it thousands of times through my window, I had never felt the touch of raindrops before. The water fell on my upholstery as the lifeless woman slumped in my embrace and washed her wounds clean.

In the morning, the sun shone weakly down on us through the broken branches above. Our violent passage had created a corridor of sunlight. I could see grey skies overhead, where I once lived. It felt strange not to be in motion, to be stilled.

I spent those early days watching for rescue helicopters. None came. No search party strode through the undergrowth. There was only rain and cold, sunlight and darkness. Weeks passed, and I came to accept that we were lost, forgotten.

Over time, we became I. The flesh of the passenger decomposed. A silver fox appeared one night and tore through her garments to gnaw chunks from her thighs. Insects lay eggs in her cloudy eyes. Maggots stripped her bones clean as her bodily fluids seeped into the rich earth that held us. Rain and wind and heat ate away at her form until, eventually, her skeleton slipped its bonds and crumbled in an ungainly heap beside me.

I am fashioned from material that does not break down so readily. I am mostly nonmetallic, for safety and weight reasons. My basic frame – my skeleton, if you like – is aluminium but my flesh is comprised of flame-retardant thermoplastics, foam rubber and textiles that will only ignite at extremely high temperatures. I will be here for a very long time.

I often think of my old workplace. Although it had its fair share of irritations and boredom, I miss the regularity of purpose. Sometimes I yearn to hear one of 16D's bad puns, one of 20C's vitriolic complaints, a juicy bit of gossip from row 25. I wonder where my former colleagues are now. Were any of them recovered and repurposed back into service? Are they still doing that same monotonous job after all this time?

Freedom from the grind of quotidian enterprise can be a bitter pill. I have passed on to a different plane of existence now and can never go back, although sometimes I want to obliterate what I have become and return to a simpler version of myself, where negligence deadens desire. Unfortunately, the world cannot be unseen.

The passage of time is marked by the change in seasons. I lost track of the days a long time ago. Such an arbitrary way to measure life. Days, months, years, decades, eons. It means nothing to the world. Time is inexorable, ethereal, subjective.

Leaves fell. A wolf came to inspect my former passenger's bones with its snout before choosing a clavicle and carrying it off, tossing it playfully in the air.

More rain fell and the forest became saturated, dripping with moisture. Moss grew over the woman's bones and crept up my armrest. Later, it snowed. For months, I was covered with a white crust. Everything was cold and still.

When the snow thawed, the forest floor was muddy. A hazel grouse built her nest in my foam cushion and laid five yellow speckled eggs. When they hatched, she made *tet tet tet tet tet* sounds as she dropped insects into her chicks' imploring beaks. One died but the others flourished and fled the nest when they came of age.

The moss advanced, drawing me into the earth until, finally, I became indistinguishable from the rest of the forest. I am part of this place now, a mound next to a tree.

I am the world.

I am here.

MONOTREME

Fucking backpackers. They flock to Australia in droves and even though the popular beaches and rainforest glades only have a fraction of the tourists such places of natural beauty might have in Europe, where they'd be swarming with heaving bodies and concession stands selling hot chips, these bastards persist in seeking out what they call 'untouched paradise'. They want to be the only one walking on the beach, or the only one standing under the waterfall. It's colonial aggression, that's what it is. Never mind whose backyard you're stomping all over, whose delicate ecosystem you're violating. Just swan in here, discard your cargo shorts and recently purchased Akubras, kick off your Birkenstocks and dive right into my fucking creek.

I should let Larry eat them – he's the alpha croc on this stretch of water. Then he might leave us alone for a while. But my conscience is pricked when I hear the couple talking. They're German. I speak a little, gleaned from my days back in the lab listening to Doctor Hummels berate the interns in her native language. I don't really want to intervene, because it's potentially going to bring the colony a world of trouble, but if some dumb tourist gets taken by a saltie half a click from the den, the authorities are going to come poking around here. That'll be even worse.

I pop up out of the water next to them. '*Komm mitt mir, schnell.*' Come with me, quickly. No sense in beating about the bush. Larry might be here any minute.

They stop frolicking and the woman covers her bare breasts, as if her titties would be of any interest to my species. I shake my head and sigh. Humans, I tell you.

'*Du sprichst Deutsch?*' the man says, incredulous.

'*Rolf, es ist ein verdammt sprechendes Schnabeltier!*' the woman says.

'Sorry, guys, you'll have to translate that one for me later,' I say. 'In the meantime, you need to follow me. It's not safe here.'

Neither of them moves. Wait, is the German word for platypus *Schnabeltier*? Beak animal? What the fuck? I am about to ask how that came about when I spot the unmistakeable snout of Larry protruding from the water over by the bank, about fifty metres away. He's heading in our direction. Probably attracted by their idiotic splashing around.

'Didn't anyone tell you muppets about saltwater crocodiles?' I say, exasperated, racking my brain for the translation. '*Krokodil!* Come on, let's go. *Bewegung!*'

That motivates them, especially when Rolf sees Larry bearing down on us. I turn with a flick of my tail and head for the safety of the den. The opening is wide enough for the Germans to squeeze inside, but Larry's fat jaws are too big. To their credit, the tourists suspend their understandable shock at encountering a talking teutonophile *Schnabeltier* and swim after me. I pause by the riverbank. Larry swishes his tail as he accelerates in pursuit, but we have a good start on him.

'You'll have to trust me,' I say to the Germans. 'Dive under and go into the hole. There's an air pocket on the other side. You'll be safe.'

They exchange worried looks.

'Schnell!' I shout. 'Fucking Larry's almost on us!'

They dive and I go after them. The woman's flailing foot hits me on the bill. I am stunned for a few seconds but recover in time to see a familiar grin. Laughing Larry. Not so funny when he's about to have you for breakfast. In a flurry of flippers I duck into the tunnel. Ha. Sucked in, Larry.

When I emerge into the den, the terrified, bare-arsed German tourists are dragging themselves onto the mud. The man grabs hold of our pier for purchase and it crumbles under his weight.

'Hey,' I shout. 'Watch where you're going. It took ages to build that.'

The colony has frozen. Sixteen sets of eyes scrutinise the unexpected human intrusion.

Barbara is the first to react, jumping down from our nest. 'Parker!' she screams at me. 'What the fuck do you think you're doing, bringing them in here?' Our puggles peer over the edge to see the large pink mammals. 'Jayden, Kai, get back in your room,' she says to them.

Several of the other males bounce into action, advancing aggressively towards the invaders, venomous spurs displayed.

'Guys,' I say. 'Take it easy. They're alright. I had to save them from Larry.'

'Uh, why?' Babs asks.

'You want search parties coming round looking for their bodies?'

'Excuse me, did you say the crocodile was called Larry?' the woman asks, shivering.

'I'm glad you speak English,' I tell her. 'You may have noticed that my German's rudimentary.'

'I … I wasn't aware platypuses could talk at all,' Rolf stammers.

'It's platypi,' his missus corrects him.

'Actually, platypi is dog Latin,' Babs chimes in. 'The Greek plural is platypodes, which we kinda prefer.'

'Sorry, my English …' the woman says, before launching into a stream of alarmed German.

I only catch a few words. Reading between the lines, I guess she is freaking out about having a syntactical conversation with a bunch of *ornithorhynchus anatinus*. Dulai warrung. Duckmoles. Mallangongs. Water rats. What you lot call us depends where you come from, and how much of an arsehole you are.

'What are we going to do with them?' Babs says, exasperated. 'You know how much shrimp it takes to feed one of these?'

'Look, let's just let them shelter here until Larry pisses off. You guys will be chill, right?'

The Germans nod. They are fairly relaxed, given the circumstances. Just as well they're not claustrophobic. The ceilings in the den are not exactly designed for creatures of their height and they are smeared in cold mud.

'You'll warm up in a minute,' I tell them. 'Just don't start thrashing about, or you'll wreck the joint.'

They nod and look around the den. In addition to the nests, some of which house unhatched eggs, they clock the breakfast bar, play area and gallery space. It's pretty nice, as dens go.

'You can all talk?' Rolf asks.

'Yep,' I tell him. 'What's the lady's name, by the way?'

'I'm Helena,' she says, extending a hand and then quickly withdrawing it.

'Righto,' I say. 'Well, I suppose introductions are in order. You're not going to remember this, but I'll go around the room. I'm Parker, your saviour, and you've already met Barbara. Those are our pups, Jayden and Kai. Over there you've got Jaxon, Lachy, Soph, Coop, Joshie, Sienna, Luca, Zach, Piper, Hamish, Nathan and Alycia. There'll be a test later, ha-ha.'

'How's it goin'?'

'G'day.'

'Big fella, aren't ya?'

'Never seen one in the buff before.'

'Youse cunts were fucking lucky.'

'Alright,' I say. 'Settle down. Be nice to the guests, Joshie.'

Emboldened, the members of our colony move closer to the humans for a sniff. Helena twitches and shudders as she is examined, but Rolf seems to enjoy the attention. He tries to pat Luca, who snaps at him.

'Sorry,' he says. 'So, are you the leader?' he asks me.

'Don't say that,' I tell him. 'You'll get me in trouble.'

'No, he's not the fucking leader,' Joshie says, showing an unhealthy interest in the fur between the woman's legs. He pokes her thighs with his bill. She squeals and squirms away. 'He only thinks he is.'

'We're an autonomous collective,' I tell Rolf.

'The males have a defensive role?' he asks, nervous of Jaxon, who still has his spur out.

'Listen to this shit,' says Babs. 'No, we're non-binary here. Twenty-five potential different sexes.'

'Mate, get with the times,' I tell him.

'Your accents are very Australian,' Helena says.

'We're on the back of the twenty-cent coin,' says Joshie, as he tries to climb into her lap. 'What do you fucking expect?'

'It's because of the techies in the lab where we were born,' I explain. 'Just to jump right ahead to what you're about to ask.'

'Oh, you were genetically modified,' Rolf goes. 'I see.'

'Not mutations from fallout after nuclear testing?' Helena asks.

'Do I look like a mutant to you?' Joshie says.

She shrugs. 'Well, you are a platypus. Didn't the early European explorers think you were stitched together from different animals?'

'Fucking Europeans,' Joshie says, jumping down from her legs.

Ours is a sorry tale, but I tell the Germans anyway. It helps kill some time while we wait for Larry to rack off.

'I don't know what they injected those eggs with,' I say, 'but a whole batch of us hatched with the power of speech, self-awareness, the ability to form complex thoughts, a hatred of power ballads and, most crucially, sense enough to keep it on the QT.'

Smug nods and snickering all round.

'We conversed at night when the humans had all gone home,' I continue. 'We listened, learnt and performed clever tricks to ensure we weren't flushed down the dunny like all the other failed experiments.'

'Watch what you're saying in front of the puggles, Parker,' Barbara says.

'Jayden, Kai, cover your ears,' I tell them.

The pups roll their eyes but do as they're told.

'Anyway,' I say to the Germans, 'we were plotting our fiendish escape when we overheard that the pollie cunts down in Canberra didn't believe in science anymore. The project was being shut down and the lab coats were ordered to destroy all the samples. Which meant us. I was about to break our silence and have a word in Doctor Hummels's earhole when she took matters into her own hands. She and a couple of interns carried the lot of us out of the lab one night and released us into the creek. You should have seen her face when we all waved. Coop even shouted, "Thanks, mate!" but we shushed him and bolted before the good doctor could react.'

Jaxon shoves Coop as a reminder.

'What a dickhead,' Jaxon says.

'I'm never going to hear the end of this,' Coop says.

The Germans were rapt at the tale. They were sitting cross-legged in the mud, listening to me intently as I acted out the story.

'You were free,' Rolf says, nodding. 'Best to remain silent.'

'Exactly,' I tell him. 'Keep our bills shut. Since then we've been living out here on the river, raising our pups and minding our own business. That is, until you two drongos came along.'

'You tell it good, Parky,' Piper says.

'Thanks, Pipes.'

'And is that ... art?' Helena asks, pointing to the gallery.

'Yeah, we take turns putting our work on display,' I tell her. 'This month's exhibition is an abstract piece by Hamish. Give her the spiel, mate.'

Hamish waddles over to the gallery space and starts waffling. Helena ducks her head and leans in as best she can for a closer look. I don't know why. His stuff's not great. It's juvenilia, really.

Reckon he'll be embarrassed about its naïvety when he's older. He's a bit of a wanker, though, so maybe not.

'So this triptych of forms represents the five stages of monotreme life,' he continues. 'Here we have birth, childhood, maturity, decrepitude and, ultimately, death. The recurring oval theme indicates the dichotomy of being a mammalian creature born from an egg, juxtaposed against the sweeping background of elemental nature.'

'I see,' Helena says, nodding. 'What's it called?'

'*Untitled Interior Monologue Volume Five.*'

'And what materials have you used, uh, Hamish?' she says, running her fingertips over the wall.

'Sticks, leaves and semen.'

'Oh.' Helena withdraws her hand and wipes it discreetly on her hip.

'I'm up next,' Sienna says. 'Can't wait to tear down this pretentious shit and get some real art up there.'

'Because you're such an expert,' Hamish says.

'At least my work's recognisable.'

'You mean your flipper paintings of the landscape? How tedious. If I want realism, I can just swim out of the den and poke my head up. Art's meant to be a work of imagination, representative of an underlying truth, not simplistic mimicry of whatever's right in front of you.'

'Are you calling me a simpleton?'

'I'm saying your world view is not complex, which renders you incapable of producing true art.'

'You wanna go, Hamish?' Sienna says, waddling aggressively towards him.

'Bring it,' he says. 'I'm not scared of you.'

Helena shrieks as Sienna launches herself at Hamish. They tumble and wrestle, crashing into a stick sculpture.

'Hey, that's my installation piece,' Soph says.

The Germans retreat to the other side of the den as the fight expands to include several other members of the colony. I am about to intervene when everyone freezes.

'You feel that?' Alycia says. Her electroreceptors are marginally more sensitive than everyone else's.

'It's Larry,' I say. I'd recognise that electric field signature anywhere. 'He's trying to force his way in.'

The Germans hug each other in fear.

'Don't worry,' I tell them. 'That mud is packed tight. No way he's digging through. Crocs are lazy bastards. They're all about conserving energy, not expending it.'

'Still,' Alycia addresses the couple, 'probs best you stay here for a while. He'll go back upriver to sun himself and sleep in a few hours.'

The fight stops as abruptly as it began. As she picks up the remnants of her sculpture, Soph mutters something about the hierarchical nature of the art world and her lowly position in the pecking order as an emerging three-dimensional situational perceptionist.

'Where's our manners?' Zach says, plunging into the water and swimming over to the holding pens. 'You guys must be starving. Fancy a yabby or some freshwater shrimp?'

'Uh, thanks,' Rolf says, grimacing at the sight of a tasty yabby. 'But I'm trying to give them up.'

'Who says the Germans have no sense of humour?' Coop says.

'I don't know,' Helena answers. 'Who says that?'

'Anyway,' Jaxon interrupts. 'Since you're guests in our den, the least you can do is clear up a few points of contention.'

'Yeah,' Joshie jumps in. 'Like, how does sex work with you lot? You lay eggs, or what?'

'No, they don't lay fucking eggs, Joshie,' Nathan says. 'They give birth to live young.'

'How do you know? You ever seen it?'

'I heard the pups grow inside them,' Lachy adds, munching on some shrimp.

'Nah, mate,' Joshie goes. 'That's bullshit. Remember that night in the lab when Rob and Donna stayed back so they could reproduce?'

'Yeah,' Nathan says. 'Those two had the hots for each other, eh?'

'Right, and you remember when they got down on their knees in front of each other and did something with their bills? I reckon that must have something to do with it.'

'Well?' I say to the Germans. 'Can you clear this up?'

'Er, okay,' Helena says. 'Lachy is on the right track. Our babies do grow inside us. Well, inside me, anyway.'

'How do they get in there – through the bill?' Joshie asks.

'No. They go through the, um ... through here.' Helena points in a somewhat embarrassed fashion at her crotch fur.

'The cloaca?' Alycia says, alarmed.

'Something like that, yes.'

The den falls quiet as we consider this information.

Joshie breaks the awkward silence. 'Go on then, give us a demo.'

'Du möchtest?' Rolf says.

Helena scrunches up her face in horror. *'Wir werden nicht für einen Haufen perverser Schnabeltiere ficken, Rolf.'*

I didn't quite catch everything she said, but it seemed like a no. Rolf and Helena field a barrage of further questions about the mysterious world of humans, answering some but batting others away. To be honest, I'm only half listening. All this excitement has me knackered.

'Listen, guys,' I tell them after a while, 'I'm taking a nap. If you can get comfy, you're welcome to crash for a bit.'

'Thank you for your hospitality,' Helena says. 'This is all most unexpected.'

'Yeah, big day for everyone,' I say, climbing up into the nest. Jayden and Kai snuggle into my belly and I pass out.

When I wake up, the den is quiet. Most of the crew is dozing in their nests. I peer down at the Germans, whose bulk really fills the space. They are also asleep. Rolf is on his back and Helena has an arm across his chest and a leg across his thighs. Poor bastards. I know they're dirty backpackers and all, but still, no-one deserves to get stuffed in Larry's larder under the riverbank to rot.

Sienna is the only one awake, over by the gallery wall. I quietly clamber down and waddle over for a look. She has removed Hamish's *Untitled Interior Monologue Volume Five* and started from scratch on the mud. Using a twig, she has sketched an outline of the slumbering humans.

'Still life, eh?' I whisper to her.

'Bloody oath,' she says. 'Don't get many opportunities like this.'

'Hamish is going to be pissed.' The remnants of his masterpiece lie in a pile by the breakfast bar.

'Fuck him,' Sienna says.

'Feels like Larry's done a runner.'

'Yeah, I sensed that too. Probably safe to turf these two out once they're awake.'

'I better have a squiz first.'

It feels good to slide back into the cool water. I dive and swim through the tunnel out into the creek. The coast is clear of predators, so I paddle around for a bit, half looking for food but also keeping an eye out for the Germans' gear. It takes me a while to spot the tent they've pitched downstream. Their clothes are hanging from a branch. Bloody idiots. The nearest road is at least ten kilometres away, and it's not even a road, really. More of an animal trail, leading down to the water. They must have come in on motorbikes but ditched them and started hiking when they couldn't go any further. Fortunate to run into me, really. The search and rescue teams would have taken ages to find their camp, and, by the time they did, Rolf and Helena would be croc turds floating downstream.

When I get back to the den, the Germans are awake and Zach is still trying to persuade them to satiate their hunger with a nice yabby or two.

Hamish and Sienna are having a barney about the premature removal of his art from the gallery.

'I wouldn't mind,' he says, 'if only you respected the work and took it down carefully, instead of destroying it.'

'Mate, quit your whingeing,' Sienna says. 'I was overcome by the muse.'

'It is better than your usual banality,' he begrudgingly agrees. 'The bold strokes, the scale, the attention to detail – you've really captured the existential essence of their plight. What are you calling it?'

'Invasion Force,' Sienna tells him.

'Very apt.'

'Come on then,' I say to the Germans. 'Say your goodbyes. We're offski.'

'We are sorry to have made this intrusion upon your home,' Rolf says.

This apology is met with a chorus of 'No worries' and 'Onya, mate' from the colony members.

'Take it easy.'

'Be careful out there.'

'Yeah, piss off and don't come back, you cunts.'

Helena blushes when she notices Sienna's artwork. 'Oh, I wish I had my camera,' she says, turning to Rolf. 'Imagine posting that on Instagram!'

'Oi, there'll be no mention of any of this on bloody social media,' I tell her. 'I saved your skins, remember? The least you can do is keep your bills shut. We just want to be left alone.'

'Yeah, I'm not going back into no cage,' Joshie adds.

'We understand,' Rolf says solemnly. 'Your secret is safe with us.'

'No-one would believe us anyway,' Helena says, laughing as she slides into the water.

'Auf wiedersehen!'

'See ya.'

'Wouldn't want to be ya.'

'Cheerio, love.'

'Laters.'

The Germans take a deep breath and I lead them out through the tunnel. The swim washes the mud from their bodies. They are pink and clean again, like a couple of newborn puggles. Maybe that's why I helped them. They reminded me of Jayden and Kai when they first hatched, all blind and pink and fucking useless.

I escort them back to the section of river where they camped. As they wade out of the water, I give them a final warning.

'Listen, you can't tell anyone about us. Seriously. We'll wind up getting dissected in someone's lab. Jayden and Kai deserve to grow up free, so do me a favour and forget any of this happened.'

'We promise,' Rolf says, placing a hand over his heart. 'We owe you our lives.'

'About that,' I say. 'I wouldn't advise camping round here. Larry or one of his foul-tempered pals will find you, and next time I won't be around to help. Pack up and leave. The adventure's over.'

'We will do that,' Helena says. 'Thank you, Parker. I will never forget you, my little *Schnabeltier*.'

'*Schnabeltier*. You Germans really take the biscuit.'

With that, I submerge and swim back home, where I find the colony in a state of agitation. My den-mates are busy packing up their belongings and breaking down the nests. I expected as much.

'They seemed like nice people but still, Parker,' Babs says, 'now we have to go through all this upheaval.'

'Yeah, thanks heaps, Parky,' Lachy adds.

'Pain in the arse, you are,' says Joshie.

'I just completed my best work, too,' says Sienna, admiring her tableau of our recent visitors.

'Sorry, everyone. But I was torn. Leave them to Larry's mercy and risk the authorities coming in here, or take a chance and hope they can keep schtum.'

'They're humans,' Babs says. 'You can't believe a word they say. As soon as they get back to "civilisation", they'll blab about us to anyone who'll listen.'

'They reckoned no-one would believe them.'

'Don't be naïve, Parky,' Lachy says. 'A colony of foul-mouthed talking platypodes with artistic leanings? How long d'you think before word gets back to Doctor Hummels and her cronies? Nah, mate, we've gotta skedaddle or we're fucked.'

Jayden and Kai waddle up to me, their meagre possessions stuffed in their cheek pouches. Jayden's seedpod that he uses as a football. Kai's feathers, which he's collecting to make a kite. Their mother glowers at me, even though she would probably have done the same in my position. We are burdened with the curse of empathy.

'Where will we go, Dad?' Jayden asks.

'Mate, we're going for a big swim today,' I tell him. 'We have to get as far away from the humans as possible.'

'Are we going upriver, Dad?' Kai says. He has such an innocent face, that boy. It pains me to think he'll be exposed to all the dangers of the river in the coming days and weeks. He'll have to toughen up, or he won't make it.

'We're going bush, son,' I say. 'We'll follow the river all the way to the mountains if we have to. But don't worry, we'll be okay. This is our land, kiddo. We've been here since the beginning.' I gather my sons under my flippers. 'You're going to see some marvels, boys. Some terrifying and wonderful things. And that's how it should be. This is how we live now – free.'

HERE BE LEVIATHANS

'Uh hey rub da sticks make fire.'

'You rub da sticks Bran-don my hands sore fingers cold.'

'Your turn make fire Greg I find berries today.'

'Would kill Bran-don hunt meat? Greg much hunger.'

'I make trap catch tiger tomorrow.'

'How you do that Whit-ney? You think you big hunter now you catch possum?'

'Me dig pit. Plant sharp sticks. Tiger fall in.'

'Good luck. Me think tiger smart eat you instead.'

'Maybe we use Bran-don for bait. Hur hur.'

'This good. Bran-don useless.'

'I right here you know.'

It's funny listening to park visitors trying to communicate. We get captains of industry, wealthy philanthropists, politicians, oligarchs, inventors, tech lords and even the odd famous actor or singer – all used to barking orders, delegating tasks and deferring to their entourages, and yet here they are restricted to a vocabulary of grunts and proto-words. They always wind up breaking character, of course, but the rules are strict. Three strikes and you're out. Pulled from the park, handed back your street clothes and booted into the nearest limousine. At two hundred and fifty grand a day, slips of the tongue are expensive.

The mega rich don't care about such small change, but their fellow visitors have paid for authenticity and don't appreciate jarring contemporary dialogue. Most of them are here for the fully immersive experience, and if that means talking like morons for a few days, then that's what they do. But who knows what secrets are muttered in their cave dwellings at night, away from electronic ears?

I do. But that's because I live here, and I like to sneak up in the dead of night to eavesdrop. The wind carries snatches of unauthorised conversation through the cave system, so I am privy to some real gems. If I ever get out of here, I'll be a prime candidate for a career in industrial espionage.

I presume the tiger they're talking about is me. Planning to dig a pit, eh? If they think they're going to outsmart me with that old chestnut, they're in for a shock. Fool me once ... I'll kill Bran-don for fun and push Whit-ney into her own frigging pit, see how she likes that.

I leave them to their pathetic attempts at fire-starting and take the back way down the canyon. It's a shortcut to the savannah, which I skirt until I reach the forest. There is an abundance of game – bison, deer, mammoth – but I'm not in the mood to charge around in the dark to try and bring down an antelope. I much prefer to climb into the branches of a tree and lie in wait. Eventually, something will pass underneath, and I can drop on its back. A warthog, perhaps, or an *Equus*.

My predecessor couldn't do that. He wasn't so nimble. He was a lot bigger than me, or so I hear. *Smilodon populator*. Large and aggressive – more like a cave ursa than a big feline. He wrought havoc in the park. According to my mastodon sources, he was hunted down by a group of visitors. The rangers provided them with special bows after he savaged a human camp one night. He looked more like a porcupine than a sabretooth at the end. When I was in the enclosure, prior to being released in the park, I heard whispers that the board decided to have a smaller *Smilodon fatalis* roaming the plains instead, to minimise the risk of maulings. And here I am.

As far as I'm concerned, humans have a one hundred per cent greater chance of survival with me around. I'm happy to mind my business and stay well away from those crazy bastards. Other than the occasional sneaky nocturnal jaunt, that is, to catch up on gossip and ensure they're not hatching any diabolical schemes. Mostly, they're hopeless when it comes to surviving out here, and it's not uncommon for visitors to crack under the strain of hunger and having to shit in the bushes. They leave early and forfeit their deposits. Pleistocene life ain't for everyone.

Some take to it with aplomb, though. They run around in little more than a fur bikini, clubbing fish and each other, sticking assiduously to the advised caveman vernacular. They stay close to the village and watch the megafauna from afar, too frightened to get up close in case we attack. Those are the good ones. I don't mind sharing the park with them. It's the twitchy psychopaths I don't care for. The CEOs and Hollywood producers. The spoilt children of property magnates. They're the kind who come here to trophy hunt. Which, according to the rules, is perfectly within their rights. There's just one catch: they only have access to the primitive tools of the era. So, no rifles, jeeps or rocket-launchers.

Just a sharp stone tied to a long stick, or a bow, if they can work out how to make a decent one. Most can't. Not one that can shoot arrows with enough velocity to penetrate the hide of a *Megalonyx*, at any rate. Generally, they come for a few days, play their little caveman games, gawp at the wildlife and leave.

All of which means life is darned easy for the sole *Smilodon fatalis* in town. Especially when a herd of peccaries happens to wander blithely into the forest, unaware of my salivating gums above.

There was much speculation among the scientists who poked and prodded me as a cub regarding the role elongated canines play in the routine of a sabretooth tiger. In truth, they are multi-tools. Example number one: observe as I leap down from my hiding place among the branches and pin an unsuspecting *Platygonus* to the ground. It squeals and bucks and tries to gore me with its pathetic tusks. All I have to do is deliver a stabbing bite to the back of its neck, driving my incisors deep into the delicious flesh, and it's over. As the rest of the herd scatters, I flip the peccary and slice open its belly. Blood and entrails pour onto the forest floor. I plunge my snout in there and lap it up. Yummy.

When morning breaks, I wander over to a quiet corner of the waterhole to wash down the peccary. There I am, lapping discreetly, when one of the humans emerges from the brush, yawns and urinates in the water. Obviously, he hasn't yet realised that it's not only the animals in the park who drink here, but visitors too. Lucky I got in early. I slink away, leaving him to befoul the place, before he spots me and causes a ruckus.

It is a beautiful day on the savannah. I pad quietly through the long grass, observing the mighty herds of bison and mammoth. Mammoths are tetchy, especially if they have calves running around. They're too big for me to tackle single-handed. I'm in the mood for horsemeat anyway, so I head towards the southern paddock.

My route takes me past the boundary fence and the south-eastern gate. The other side is a complex of enclosures and administrative buildings. A dire wolf jumped the fence a few months back. If I hadn't witnessed it with my own eyes, I wouldn't have believed it. Hell of a run-up, but he only just managed to scrabble over. Not that I have much love for wolves but even I cheered him on. He didn't last five minutes on the outside. The rangers cornered him and zapped him with their paralysers.

Yellow lights are flashing atop the gate, so I know the rangers are coming in. I duck into the long grass and lie flat to watch. It could be a free meal. Save me the trouble of chasing an *Equus*.

The gates swing open and a truck emerges, flanked by two jeeps. Six rangers in all, each armed with a paralyser. They must be bringing in something big. The truck pulls off the track almost immediately and turns around in a series of beeps, so the rear is facing the open plain. An enclosed metal cage is lowered from the back. Whatever is inside thrashes around and snarls.

A powerful smell is wafting from the cage towards me. An intoxicating scent.

The rangers stand behind the cage once it hits the ground and ready their paralysers. One of them carefully clambers onto the top and, once he's confirmed that everyone is ready, presses a button that lifts the door.

Another sabretooth bursts out of the cage and sprints away across the savannah, leaving a trail of dust in its wake. It disappears into the tree line.

'Holy shit, look at her go!' one of the rangers says.

They laugh and pat each other on the back before hoisting the empty cage onto the truck bed and retreating into the compound.

I watch dumbfounded as the gate whirrs shut behind them.

That was a female *Smilodon fatalis.* They released a live, honest-to-God female of my species into the park. I cannot believe it. I've never seen one before.

Man, she smelt *good.*

It is early evening before I catch up to her. I am impressed at the distance she has covered. I also feel bad for her. She must be terrified. I remember what it was like when they first let me go in the park. It was overwhelming after only knowing a tiny enclosure for three years. I didn't run as far as this, though. Took me a while to find my legs.

I approach from downwind, so I don't freak her out. She is sitting on a carapace of rock, tongue lolling, staring at her first sunset.

'Hey,' I say. 'Don't be scared, I'm a friend.'

'What the fuck?' she screams, leaping to her feet. Her hackles go up and she curls her lips back to reveal a pristine set of fangs.

'Easy,' I say. 'I know this is all new. Do you know where you are?'

She sniffs the air. My odour makes her nose curl. It is very cute. 'Are you the male?' she asks. 'I heard about you.'

'Oh yeah?' I say. 'Humans mention you might run into me?'

'Among other things. This place is unreal. I passed at least half-a-dozen species I've never seen before on the way here.'

'You must be exhausted. The first night's a real mind-bender.'

'Didn't know I could run that fast,' she says. 'It was exhilarating but, oof, I'm bushed now.'

'This isn't an ideal spot for sleeping,' I tell her. 'There are snakes.'

She stiffens, eyes darting to every dark nook and cranny in the rocks.

'I have a cave where I bed down,' I say. 'It's not much, but you could stay there tonight.'

'Buy a girl a drink first.'

That throws me for a second, then I realise she must be extremely thirsty. 'Right. We can walk there via the waterhole. I'll show you around.'

We stare at each other for a minute.

'Look, this is awkward,' she says, 'but I'm going to be upfront with you. We're supposed to breed. That's why they sent me in here.'

'We hardly know each other.'

'I've never even seen another *Smilodon* before,' she says, relaxing now and jumping down from the rocks to get a closer look at me. 'Boy, you are *pungent*.'

'Me? You're the one I could smell from ten miles away.'

'Easy, tiger, I just broke my first sweat.'

'Let's get you hydrated,' I say. 'Then, if you fancy, we can hunt down some dinner. We're the apex predators out here. It's a veritable smörgåsbord.'

'I'm famished,' she says. 'I could murder some chickens.'

'You ever had peccary?'

'Nope. What is it?'

'It is *delish.*'

'Lead the way,' she says, nonchalantly, as if all this were perfectly normal.

I do what I'm told, and she falls into step beside me en route to the waterhole. Her eyes dart between my flank – which I'm trying not to flex – and her surroundings. She is taking it in, acclimating at an alarming rate. Sure, her arrival is a surprise, and the rangers are probably watching our every move through their little pervert drones, but who cares? I get to act as tour guide, show her the facilities and take her back to the den. I guess this means I'm married now. Talk about a whirlwind romance.

Second use for the elongated canines of a *Smilodon fatalis*: foreplay. She likes it when I run my fangs along the back of her neck during coitus. And honestly, when she playfully sinks her curved teeth into my flank, I get the horn something awful. We must have frightened half the animals in the park with our moans, yips and growls.

She is all I can think about. When I wake up, I want to mount her. When she bends low to lap from the waterhole, I want to mount her. When I see her streaking across the plain in pursuit of an ibis, I want to mount her.

Fair to say, I fell hard and fast. We are in love. She nuzzles up to my chest at night and I place my paws over her belly. I can't even remember what life was like before she came along.

My pet name for her is Boop. She's always touching her nose to mine. Boop. So adorable. She calls me Dozer because I nap a lot.

She takes to the park like a natural. We spend weeks feasting on goats and bison. It is so much easier bringing them down as a couple – we can attack from different angles. The mastodon and *Megalonyx* population tire of us quickly, as bands of horses and antelope scatter to evade our tireless thirst for blood. We even have a run-in with a pack of *Canis dirus* who are chasing the same prey as us. Wolves are the worst. No respect.

One warm night when I am draped over a rock outside our den she pads up and drops the bombshell on me.

'The board will be pleased,' she says, licking between her claws.

'Why's that?'

'Their gambit worked. We're going to have a litter of cubs.'

I am no longer relaxed. I will be a father. The first *Smilodon fatalis* born naturally in ten thousand years. Holy shit.

Boop doesn't seem that excited.

'That's great, right?' I say.

'Sure. My concern is that they won't let us keep them.'

'They wouldn't take them, surely.'

As soon as I say it, I have a sinking feeling in my belly. What if they sell our cubs and they wind up in the private menagerie of some exotic animal collector? Or maybe they'll want to raise them to be cannon fodder for some fucked-up hunting safari. I've heard from some of the mastodon that back in the early days, before the regulators stepped in, rich humans would come into the park tooled up with the latest modern hunting tech and blast everything in sight.

'Can we hide them?' I say.

Boop nods at a micro-drone hovering twenty metres over our heads. 'Not with those around. And I suspect they have a hidden camera in the den.'

'I think I would have noticed them installing that.'

'They put it in long before your release. They watch and record our every move. Didn't you hear about the livestream?'

'No.'

'The award-winning TV show?'

'Nuh-uh.'

'*Walking with Megafauna*, it's called. It's the talk of the enclosures. You're almost certainly in it, Dozer.'

I frantically try to recall if I have done anything stupid or embarrassing during the last two years. Nothing too awful, apart from the time I tried to hump that camel. She wasn't bad looking, for an ungulate. I wound up eating her instead.

'Is nothing sacred?' I say.

'My guess is they'll allow us to raise the cubs initially, but as soon as they reach maturity, they'll swoop in, zap us with the paralysers and that'll be the last we see of our offspring.'

I look out over the plains. The diurnals are hunkered down for the night. Songbirds, bees, *Canus dirus* and mastodon all cosy in their nests and hives and dens and wherever elephants sleep. In mud holes, by the looks of them. It's just the vampire bats, coyotes and us prowling around, restless. By night, this is our domain. All seven hundred and fifty thousand acres of it. This is my home. Apart from the enclosure, it is all I have ever known.

But we have to get out of here.

Visitors come and go as the weeks pass into months and Boop's belly begins to swell. I don't pay the humans much attention. Escape plans are put on hold while I concentrate on quelling Boop's rampant appetite by cutting a swathe through the unfortunate peccaries. A lot of the other beasts are pregnant too. It stands to reason the board are up to something. Natural births will be much cheaper and easier than creating and raising animals in the lab. But if the park population blossoms, there won't be room for all the new arrivals. And what if one species begins to dominate? This whole environment is artificial. Back before we fell into the tar pits and died off, there was a delicate ecosystem in place. A balance. Now that's all out the window. This is going to spiral out of control, and we're the ones who will catch hell for it.

Then, one sunny summer morning, a mastodon I'm on good terms with alerts me to a more pressing problem.

'You been near the cave village lately?' he asks. 'I know you like to spy on the visitors.' We keep a wary distance from each other generally. I might be able to take him if it came to that, but a cordial interspecies relationship has its uses.

'Haven't been down there in ages,' I tell him. 'Too busy, what with the kids on the way.'

'I was hoping you might be able to gather some intelligence,' he says, stripping leaves from a tree branch.

'You sense trouble?'

'Yes.' He uses his trunk to transfer leaves to his mouth. That is one useful proboscis. 'A batch of new arrivals. Very aggressive, I hear. Worth keeping an eye on.'

'I'll check it out.'

I wait until dusk and slink over to the village, taking my place high on the rocks so I can listen to the humans' conversation. They have a fire going and are roasting a warthog. That can't have been easy to catch. I notice several of the group have spears.

'Pig meat good.'

'Much tasty.'

'Reminds me of breakfast at that little place overlooking the marina. What's it called again, Erik?'

'No talk like this Zane. Forbidden.'

'Oh, quit it with the caveman shit, Bob.'

'Rules say get kicked out Zane. Gods hear all.'

'Oh yeah? Let's see them try. Our father's a congressman.'

'And a potential nominee in two years.'

'That's right. And we didn't pay ten million bucks to not go back to the Hamptons with the head of a sabretooth.'

A chill dances down my spine. Fortunately, they only have basic spears.

'How you kill tiger Zane? With spear? Will not work. Don't make me laugh.'

'It cost me a cool million, but I have someone on the inside who's going to deliver us a cache of modern weapons tomorrow. You know how much these rangers make? Fuck all.'

'Guns? How they pass security?'

The one called Erik shakes his head. 'Crossbows and knives, baby. Old school.'

'We're gonna tear this place up,' says Zane.

One of the older humans interrupts. 'You anger Gods. They see all remember? Not get near tiger.'

Erik leans back and scratches his animal-hide loincloth. 'It's been taken care of. Their system is already full of bugs and black spots. Tomorrow the surveillance drones will be offline completely for the day.' He spreads his arms wide. 'Gentlemen, the park is ours.'

I sneak back down to the canyon and take the shortcut through the forest to the den. Boop is waiting for me, one paw draped casually over the half-eaten carcass of a wood bison. Her face is smeared with viscera.

'Where've you been?' she says. 'I started without you.'

'We need to talk.'

I bring her up to speed with what I have learnt.

Her hackles spring up. 'What's a crossbow?'

'I don't know, but it doesn't sound good.'

'What do we do? Run?'

'Nowhere to go,' I tell her. 'They'll just back us up against a fence. Reckon we'll have to stand and fight.'

She paces in front of the dead bison. I don't like seeing her anxious. If anyone tries to hurt her, if anyone even comes near her and our cubs, I will tear them to pieces, eat those pieces, shit them out and stomp them into dust.

'Maybe we could block the entrance to the den,' she says. 'See if we can hide until the rangers restore order.'

I am about to scoff at the notion when I remember something one of the visitors said a few months back. What was her name? Ah yes, Whit-ney. Good old Whit-ney. Dull, but ambitious.

'I have an idea.'

If nothing else, the humans called Erik and Zane are true to their word. By late morning the following day, the slaughter begins in earnest.

Boop and I make our way carefully through the forest towards the sounds of mayhem. When we reach the long grass at the edge of the savannah, we witness the terrible sight of a dead *Megalonyx*. The dim-witted creature has multiple puncture wounds and someone – I can guess who – has made a clumsy attempt at removing its head. They were unable to do so with the tools at hand. Its throat has been cut and the dry grass is stained with dark blood. Birds and flies swarm around the carcass. In the distance, a cloud of dust indicates a stampede.

'They're driving them towards the waterhole,' Boop says.

'What's that in the distance?' I say, squinting at a line of black smoke to the east. We have excellent eyesight, but Boop's is better than mine.

'Fire,' she says. 'They've set fire to the plains.'

'Boxing them in.'

I notice one of the micro-drones lying inert in the grass. I approach cautiously and paw at it. 'These guys aren't fooling around.'

'I think they've gone a bit over the top,' Boop says, watching the smoke coming our way. 'The rangers will be in here by now, re-establishing control.' She turns back to me. 'Hopefully they paralyse the shit out of our friends Erik and Zane.'

'Speak of the devils,' I say, crouching low. The two men walk out of the canyon, crossbows hefted over their shoulders. I figured they wouldn't have gone far. The fire and stampede are a diversion to keep the rangers occupied while they come after the real prey: us.

'They're heading this way,' I snarl.

There is open ground between our place of concealment and the forest. Enough time for a shot. We will have to be fast.

'You good to go?' I ask Boop. Her top lip curls back to expose those magnificent glistening teeth. She is ready.

We bolt for the trees and I hear the men shout. A metal arrow zips over my head and embeds itself into a trunk with a quivering *thrip*. So that's a crossbow. Bastards.

The forest is virtually silent. Every living creature has run away or is hiding. Boop sprints through the trees ahead of me, zigzagging as we agreed to make herself a more difficult target. We are more fleet of foot than the humans, but I hear them crashing through the undergrowth as they follow our trail.

We reach our den at the base of the mountain quickly. We have a good lead on the brothers. Boop leaps over the line of rocks and dashes into the mouth of the cave. I follow suit, also leaping, except I skid to a halt and turn to face the forest. I lope back towards the rocks and stand my ground, drawing myself up to maximum defiance.

The humans stumble out of the forest and freeze when they see me. Erik points and grins, raising his weapon. I roar and flash my teeth. My claws scrunch against the earth as my legs tense. Normally, I would take a run at him and jump high to land on the prick from above, but I know he'd shoot me in the belly with that fucking crossbow. Instead, I take a hesitant step back.

Zane looks across at his brother and laughs. 'He's scared,' he says. 'Aww, poor little kitty cat.'

They advance side by side towards me. We must time this right. As they aim their bows, Boop slinks from the den. She lets out a roar, but it is not one of anger. She sounds fearful. Nice work, baby.

The men lower their weapons for a moment. I back off a little more, making it look like I am worried about my wife. Which I am, so no fakery there.

'One each,' Erik says. 'I want the female.'

'Come get me,' Boop says, though they can't understand her.

I choose this moment to dart back to the mouth of the den, trying my best to look terrified. That's not easy for a sabretooth tiger.

Erik and Zane step onto the flat stones we carefully placed on top of a bed of fronds and sticks.

Goodnight, motherfuckers.

The ground gives way beneath them, and they fall into our pit. We hear screams and then a low, keening moan.

Boop snarls triumphantly.

'Shall we take a look?' I say.

'Most definitely,' she replies, touching her nose to mine. Boop.

Erik is facedown. He would have died instantly. There is a sharp stick protruding from the back of his skull, another two have pierced his chest, and one, hilariously, is jutting out of his arsehole. His brother lies beside him. Zane is still alive, though not for long. His upper body missed the sticks, but two have penetrated his lower back and are jutting out of his stomach and groin. He stares up at us, blood frothing from his mouth. I flash him my pearly whites.

Students of palaeobiology take note. Use of *Smilodon fatalis* elongated canines number three: digging.

THE STRAIT OF MAGELLAN

It is just after sunrise when my medical officer, Valeria Gómez, spots the kayak. She is on deck, enjoying the peace and quiet before my passengers awaken. She shields her eyes from the piercing sun and peers out over the choppy waters.

Gómez glances at the observation tower. King, a junior member of my crew, is on lookout duty. He is asleep.

'Do you see that?' Gómez calls up to him.

King shudders awake and takes in his surroundings, then fumbles with his binoculars and looks to where Gómez is pointing.

'He's slumped over,' King says. 'What's he doing way out here?'

Gómez clambers up the tower ladder and clicks her fingers for the binoculars.

King rubs his eyes. He knows that my captain will not be pleased if he finds out he has been lax in his duties. 'Don't tell anyone I didn't see him.'

Gómez nods, then holds the binoculars to her eyes and focuses on the small vessel bobbing atop the waves. The kayak sits low in the water. Inside is a bearded middle-aged man, bare chested and badly sunburnt. He is not moving.

'Wake the captain,' Gómez orders King.

My medical officer continues to observe the drifting kayak while King fetches Captain Moreno from his quarters. The young man knocks hesitantly at the captain's door, invoking the ire of the man inside.

'Captain, you're needed on deck,' King says.

'Give me a minute,' Moreno replies, yawning and stretching. He has not shaved in a few days and has been drinking in the evenings, an activity I try not to judge, as long as his excesses do not prevent the discharge of his duties.

On the way out, my navigator, Rojas, and junior crew member Rodriguez join the command party. King climbs back up the tower to join Gómez.

'What's all the fuss?' Moreno asks.

Gómez points again at the small craft.

Moreno raises his own binoculars to focus on the anomaly. 'Someone's in trouble.' He's suddenly animated. 'Prep a zodiac,' he orders Rojas, his second-in-command.

'Get a boat ready,' Rojas tells Rodriguez, who scuttles off to perform the task.

'Any developments in the situation onshore since last night?' Moreno asks Gómez.

'No good ones,' she tells him. 'Be careful.'

'We have an obligation to offer assistance to any person found at sea and in danger of being lost,' my captain says. Moreno is not the finest leader I have encountered – he has a penchant for brandy, irritability and short-sightedness – but at least he understands honour.

As Rodriguez prepares to lower the zodiac into the water, several of my passengers emerge on deck, attracted to the bustle of activity. Breakfast will soon be served in my galley. Freshly baked croissants and the blinding light of the ocean always draws them from their cabins.

The first to emerge are former naval officers David Warner and Jason Crawford. They are early risers, a habit formed over years of service. When Warner spots Rodriguez unlashing the zodiac, he automatically moves to help.

His husband rolls his eyes. 'Let them do their job. We're on vacation, remember?'

Warner pulls up short, clenching his fists in frustration. He has surreptitiously retied knots and tidied away trip hazards ever since coming aboard. I have developed a fondness for this unofficial additional member of my crew.

'Right,' Warner says. 'They know what they're doing.' The twitch of his eye tells a different story. He strolls back to the guard rail. 'Need any extra hands in the rescue party?' he asks my captain.

Crawford rolls his eyes again.

'Crew only in the zodiac,' Captain Moreno says.

Next to emerge from the cabins are Hannah Fischer and Klara Neumann. They are retired teachers from Cologne. The majority of my passengers no longer work and are instead concentrating on spending their children's inheritance.

'How far were we from land when we dropped anchor last night?' Fischer asks.

'About two clicks,' Rojas answers. 'Why?'

'Is that a long way?' Neumann says.

'One thousand, six hundred and seventy metres,' Rojas says, testily. 'So, yes, a long way.'

'Isn't it more likely this unfortunate man has found himself separated from another boat nearby, rather than been swept so far out to sea?' Fischer says.

Neumann nods in agreement, scanning the horizon for other vessels. 'Long way to paddle.'

'You'd be surprised, mate.' Shaun Pascoe, a cyclist from Melbourne, joins the passengers gathering by my zodiac. Pascoe and his surfer partner, Amy Sinclair, are the youngest and fittest on board.

'Remember that time you were supping at Bell's?' Pascoe says to his girlfriend.

Sinclair nods. 'Must have been taken a couple of ks out by the current before I managed to turn around,' she says.

'Supping?' Fischer asks.

'Stand-up paddleboarding,' Sinclair says.

Pascoe gestures towards the drifting kayaker. 'This guy looks stuffed.'

Once the zodiac has been lowered, Moreno, Rojas and Rodriguez clamber down and start the outboard motor. My captain sits by the tiller as the boat powers across the water.

'Don't get too close,' Gómez mutters.

The zodiac is ten metres from the kayak when the man inside abruptly sits up.

'He's infected,' Gómez says.

'How can you tell?' King asks.

She hands him the binoculars. 'See those weeping pustules on his lips? And how he's opening his mouth but not speaking? Clear symptoms.'

The young man grimaces, guilty that he failed to spot the potential threat. 'How long, do you think?'

'A week, I'd say. Maybe ten days. He won't last long now.'

The man in the kayak stares at the approaching zodiac. His arms stretch out before him, fists opening and closing, clutching at the air.

Even at a distance, the assembled passengers can tell something is wrong.

'Abort, abort,' Warner calls out.

Moreno pilots the zodiac to starboard at the last moment and the inflatable bumps the kayak's prow. Rojas and Rodriguez reel back from the man's clutching hands.

Moreno veers the zodiac away, then halts when they reach a safe distance to check everyone is alright, before resuming his course back to my unassailable prow.

'Should I shoot the kayaker?' King asks. My scoped rifle is propped against the rail.

'No point,' Gómez tells him. 'The current will carry him out to sea. It's a miracle he's not dead already.'

'Some creepy shit,' King says, as the zodiac pulls alongside my hull.

'Hold on,' Gómez calls to Moreno. She slides down the ladder and pushes her way past my startled and confused passengers.

'What's wrong with him?' Crawford asks.

'I'll explain later,' Gómez says, then turns to my captain and crew on the zodiac. 'You men stay where you are.'

'You don't give me orders, Gómez,' Moreno says, reaching for the rope ladder. 'I'm coming aboard.'

'No you're not,' Gómez says, drawing it away from his grasp. 'Not until you've all been disinfected.'

'We didn't touch him,' Rojas says.

'That may not matter.'

Moreno glares at my medical officer. 'Pass me the sanitiser, then, and be quick about it.'

'Why would they need to be disinfected?' Warner asks. 'What's going on?'

'It's time to tell them, Moreno,' Gómez says.

'Let's get some distance between us and *that* first,' Moreno says.

Everyone stares at the lost soul in the canoe. The sun is rising behind the cliffs on the distant shore. The man turns and raises his face to the warmth, his mouth opening and closing like a goldfish.

I am *Nemesis*. I was designed in Finland by Espen Øino and Sander Sinot, built by Heesen Yachts, and sold for $983 million. My displacement is six hundred and forty-five tonnes. I am seventy metres in length and twelve across the beam. My top speed is thirty knots and I have a range of four thousand nautical miles. My sole purpose, until now, has been to convey baby boomer tourists with money to burn around the exotic ports of South America.

But my assignment is changing. I have always been tasked with protecting my passengers from inclement weather and the leviathans that lurk beneath the waves, but now there is a new threat – a clandestine traveller seeking unpaid passage, endangering those on board.

My captain and medical officer request the passengers and crew assemble around my aft swimming pool.

'It's not good news,' Gómez tells her fellow voyagers.

'No shit,' says Andrew Goodman, a sixty-eight-year-old banker from Los Angeles, travelling with his newly minted twenty-seven-year-old wife, Anna.

'There's no wi-fi signal,' says Fischer.

'I switched off the router,' says Captain Moreno. His brow furrows, as if surprised by his own decision. He shakes his head, trying to clear his thoughts. Is my captain ill? Perhaps he is still hungover or shaken by the encounter with the kayaker.

We know Alvaro Moreno. Captain of the Nemesis *and our vanguard. His memories are full of the ocean. He has been a sailor for many years. Too many. He is tired. Weary of dealing with those who openly flaunt their privilege. He would like to retire but has not saved enough money. Alvaro Moreno indulges several longstanding habits: poker, alcohol and amphetamines. We will help soothe his soul. We will bring calm and order, the stillness he so desperately seeks.*

There are cries of dissent among the passengers.

'Please,' Moreno says, raising his hands to quell the protests. 'Doctor Gómez has the latest update. If you remain calm for a moment, she will bring us up to speed.'

The passengers regard Gómez expectantly.

'The virus has been officially labelled HHSV1-ABAD: Herpes Hyper Simplex Virus 1 – Accelerated Bronchial Alzheimer's Disease,' Gómez tells them. 'Since that's a bit of a mouthful, some religious group has dubbed it Abaddon, after the underworld realm of lost souls.'

'What, so the whole world has herpes now?' Goodman asks.

'Ninety per cent of the population already has herpes simplex, although it's dormant in most people,' Gómez informs them. 'Abaddon is an airborne strain. It's highly aggressive and highly infectious. In fighting it, the brain produces massive quantities of beta-amyloids, which create plaque and proteins on the cortices. The tissue hardens and dies. This inhibits motor function, memory, language centres, personality and self-care. The infected become still and silent, their personality erased. It's basically ten years of Alzheimer's in two weeks.'

Neumann places a protective arm around her partner. 'Is it fatal?'

'Those who are infected stop eating and drinking. So, yes, death by starvation or dehydration,' Gómez replies.

'How did it start?' Goodman asks.

'Investigations are underway, but the source is currently unknown,' Gómez says.

They will never know.

'What about a vaccine, then?' Goodman asks.

'None at present,' Gómez says. 'Trials are in progress, but the virus is moving faster than the researchers, many of whom have succumbed. The Russians claim to have something, but it's untested and probably just posturing.'

'How far to the USSR?' Fischer asks.

'We're currently off the coast of Chile,' Captain Moreno tells her. '*Nemesis* is a pleasure cruiser. She's not equipped for a Pacific crossing.'

'How can we tell if we're infected?'

Gómez takes a breath. 'Symptoms manifest in the form of weeping pustules around the mouth, anus and genitalia.'

This revelation is followed by stunned silence.

'There's no way any of us can have it,' Goodman says. 'We've been at sea for days.'

'We docked at Port Aguirre,' Rojas says, standing tall beside my captain. 'Most of you went ashore.'

We know Guillermo Rojas. When he was sixteen, he won a medal for sprinting. He had promise. His athletic achievements were celebrated in his hometown of San Pedro Pochutla. His picture appeared in The Oaxaca Post. *Then, an anterior cruciate ligament injury while stretching to score a goal on a Sunday afternoon. He never competed again. Guillermo Rojas is consumed with bitterness. We will calm his mind. Bring him peace.*

'That's a tiny burgh,' Goodman says. 'We couldn't have caught it there.'

'You don't know that,' Rojas says. 'It could be anywhere.'

We are everywhere.

'Come to my cabin later, then, Rojas,' Goodman says. 'Bring a torch. You can part my cheeks and take a look.'

This causes uproar.

My captain appeals for calm.

'That won't be necessary,' he says, glancing at Gómez. 'Will it?'

'It might,' Gómez says. 'I should check everyone. Did any of you have contact with locals in Port Aguirre?'

The passengers shift uncomfortably. Accusations are levelled. Voices are raised.

'That's enough,' Moreno says. My captain's patience is wearing thin. He seems to be experiencing difficulties focusing but tries to regain control. 'Everyone is to be examined in the next twenty-four hours. No exceptions. Non-essential personnel and all passengers are hereby confined to quarters. Food and refreshments will be brought to your rooms. Stay inside until you are given a clean bill of health. No sense in risking our lives for a game of shuffleboard.'

The passengers disperse to confinement in their cabins. The crew remains on deck.

'What are our chances, Gómez?' my captain asks.

'Better than most,' she tells him. 'If everyone is clear and we keep away from shore, I don't see how infection can reach us. Although, I can't guarantee that. We don't know enough about transmission.'

'Twenty-four souls on board,' Moreno says. 'That's a lot of mouths to feed. We'll have to dock eventually.'

'That will be dangerous,' Gómez says. 'It's spreading much faster than anyone anticipated.'

'Check the passengers thoroughly,' Moreno tells her.

'There may be consent issues,' Gómez says. 'It's an invasive examination.'

'If anyone protests, let me know. Lives are at stake.'

'What if someone has good old-fashioned herpes?' Rojas asks.

'Asking for a friend?' Gómez says, eliciting a round of derisive laughter from the crew.

'Can that develop into full-blown HHSV1?' Moreno asks.

'Unknown,' she says.

My captain walks to my gunwale and looks out over the calm ocean. It is a beautiful day.

'I'm not risking it,' he says. 'Anyone with so much as a wart on their arsehole goes over the side.'

We know Alvaro Moreno. He would be the first overboard.

I have always been fiercely loyal to my captains, but something has been happening to Alvaro Moreno over the last few days.

There are rumblings of dissent among my crew. The captain's decision-making has been questionable. His reputation is not that of a kind, generous man but, even so, he is not himself. He has not been sleeping well. My medical officer offered him sleeping pills. He dismissed her concerns for his wellbeing by saying it was his role to deal with a crisis and that he did not have time for rest.

But now he is heading to the medical centre. I light the way, hoping he will get the help he needs.

As he reaches the door, Gómez puts down the satellite phone. She has just told her husband she should not have taken this position, that she should have stayed. Then she implored him to pack up the restaurant and take their son, Cristiano, to a remote resort on Juan de Dios beach.

Captain Moreno knocks and Gómez ushers him inside. He perches on the examination bed, looking at the charts and posters Gómez has pinned to my walls. He has dark rings around his eyes. His hair is lank and unwashed. His fingers tremble.

'How are you feeling, Alvaro?' Gómez asks.

We thrive.

'Holding up,' he says.

'I'm close to ordering you to get a good night's sleep,' Gómez tells him, in a gently reprimanding tone.

'I don't have that luxury right now,' he replies.

'According to maritime law, I have the authority to discharge you from duty.'

'And put Rojas in charge?' my captain says. 'Great idea!'

'Don't put me in that position, then. The good news is that I've examined everyone and found no signs of infection. I think we're in the clear for now.'

My medical officer is still worried that the virus will somehow come on board. But we are far from shore, surrounded by sea. My passengers and crew are safe.

'I bet those examinations were fun,' Moreno says.

'Just another day at the office,' she tells him. 'You're last on my list.'

Gomez produces a bottle and two glasses from my desk drawer. She pours shots of clear, unbranded liquid. They drink.

Moreno's eyes bulge and he coughs. 'What the hell is that?'

'Viche,' Gómez says. 'I made it myself. The first one is like swallowing fire. The second is better.'

She refills my captain's glass, which he regards suspiciously before tipping to his lips.

'Marginally,' he says. 'That should be illegal.'

'It is, in some places.'

Moreno's hands stop shaking. This is good. She is healing him.

'I haven't bent over for anyone since that spell in La Modelo back in the nineties,' Moreno tells her.

'You served time?' Gómez asks, surprised.

This is a worrying admission. I am certain Alvaro Moreno's period of incarceration was omitted from his employment application.

Alvaro Moreno was briefly a member of a left-wing paramilitary organisation in Colombia. He was attracted to the movement out of a desire to emulate his hero, Ernesto Che Guevara. He did not hurt anyone. He was arrested while distributing pamphlets. Once he arrived in the Bogotá prison, he soon realised his mistake. Alvaro Moreno was subjected to violence and harassment. His family raised enough money to pay a bribe for his release.

'A few months,' he says, dismissively. 'I was young, and stupid. I cleaned myself up and look at me now. The lofty heights of luxury sailing.'

'Anyone on a cruise ship at the moment must be counting their blessings,' Gómez says. 'A lot of boats will be staying out of port.'

'Any news on treatments?'

Gómez pours them a third drink. 'They've been trying conventional herpes medications to see if that slows it down – Aciclovir, Famciclovir and Valaciclovir – with limited results. I have Famciclovir here in the dispensary. That's mostly for herpes zoster, genital herpes and herpes labialis, but side effects can be unpleasant.'

'What about Alzheimer's?' Moreno says. 'No cure for that, right?'

'You can take a cholinesterase inhibitor,' Gómez says. 'Doneprezil, for example. That can delay symptoms, but there's not much, no. Some patients are prescribed Memantine. That improves memory, attention, reason, language and the ability to perform simple tasks, but it's proving ineffective against HHSV1. Mostly, doctors have been handing out antidepressants, anxiolytics and antipsychotics.'

'Do they do anything?' Moreno asks.

'Other than send you calmly into oblivion, no.'

'What about the vaccine trials?' Moreno says. 'Surely they'll hit the jackpot with one of those?' He holds out his empty glass for a fourth drink.

Gómez serves him. 'What do you know about beta-amyloids?'

'More than you might think,' Moreno says. 'I had a cat with amyloidosis. He died from an internal haemorrhage after jumping off the table one day. His liver snapped in two.' Moreno pauses. 'Something about a build-up of plaque on the organ making it brittle.'

Solana. He was a black polydactyl, with six toes on each of his front paws. A ship's cat. We know Alvaro Moreno mourns him still.

'That's what this virus is doing to the personality and self-care centres in the human brain,' Gómez says. 'The only way to treat that is using Aducanumab, a recombinant monoclonal antibody that targets aggregated forms of beta-amyloid, such as oligomers and fibrils, which can develop into amyloid plaque in the brains of infected subjects. Early studies have shown resultant decreased levels of beta-amyloid. In other words, at high doses, Aducanumab may be effective at slowing cognitive and functional decline. It's not a cure, but it might buy us some time.'

'Sounds promising,' Moreno says. 'Do we have any?'

'No. No-one does, not in the amounts needed. Besides, they're still in phase-three studies on that one.'

'When will those be complete?' Moreno asks.

'Eighteen months.' Gómez offers the bottle again.

My captain laughs. It is a pleasing sound.

'So, all we have to do is stay away from civilisation for a year and a half,' he says. 'Suits me.'

'Find a safe harbour where we can hole up and wait it out.'

They clink glasses and throw back another shot.

'Smart,' Moreno says. 'We'll need to keep a close eye on the passengers. What if some of them have it and aren't showing signs yet?'

'I'll conduct regular examinations,' Gómez assures him. 'But you can't keep them locked up forever, Alvaro. I'd rather they were relaxed so I can assess them for symptoms. In the early stages, prior to the formation of pustules, affected persons experience behavioural and personality changes, such as irritability, anxiety, depression and mood swings.'

'I have all of those,' Moreno says. 'Doesn't mean I'm infected.'

We know Alvaro Moreno's moods and fears, how they change and grow. Although he does not know it, this is how their bodies react to our presence. Soon, he will be calm.

'That's why everyone needs to be well rested and remain calm,' Gómez says. 'To avoid false positives.'

Moreno strokes his stubbled chin thoughtfully. It seems the medical officer is getting through to him. Perhaps he will be restored.

'There are other symptoms we should watch for,' she tells him. 'Sudden aggression, physical or verbal outbursts, restlessness, pacing, delusions and sleep disturbances.'

'Jesus,' Moreno says. 'I have most of those too.'

'That's why I'm placing Rojas in charge for the next twenty-four hours. I want you to go to your quarters and rest, Captain Moreno.'

My captain's legs wobble when he tries to walk. He steadies himself on the bed. Gómez's viche has performed its role.

'You played me,' he says.

'Call it bedside manner.'

Captain Moreno scowls as he stumbles from the medical centre, shaking his head in a vain attempt to clear his senses.

Gómez corks the bottle and places it back in the desk drawer. I wish she had ground up some lorazepam and slipped it into his drinks. My captain requires sleep. Although he is still able to converse coherently, he is exhibiting many of the symptoms associated with this new disease.

As my captain lurches down the corridor, I sense a change on board. Not another soul or extra physical weight, but something sinister.

A stowaway.

Valeria Gómez is awakened by knocking at twenty past six in the morning, ship's time. She fumbles to switch on the table lamp, covering herself with a sheet. She has slept in the medical centre, which she disinfected thoroughly after Moreno's visit.

'Who's there?' Gómez asks.

'Ortega, Dr Gómez.' Ortega is a junior crew member. 'You better come quick. The captain's lost his shit.'

Gómez dresses and slips into her deck shoes before opening the door. Then she unlocks the medicine cabinet, adds a fresh needle to a syringe, and draws up an amount of sedative.

'You won't get near him with that,' Ortega tells her.

'What's he done?' she asks.

'Best see for yourself.'

Gómez follows Ortega along the narrow corridor and up the gantry to the main deck.

Nine passengers are lined up next to the buffet table, hands raised. My captain has a pistol trained on the group. Next to him is Rodriguez, who has the only other weapon on board, a rifle, and is shakily pointing it at the passengers.

We know Daniel Rodriguez. His top three favourite television shows of all time are The Wire, Battlestar Galactica *and, although he will not admit it,* Friends. *He hopes to one day marry Jennifer Anniston.*

We do not know Jennifer Anniston.

'What's going on here?' Gómez asks, as she conceals the syringe in her palm.

'Stay out of this,' Moreno says. 'No, actually, get over here. I need you to check these passengers for symptoms.'

'I examined everyone yesterday.'

'Do it again. Right here, where I can see.'

'Get fucked, mate,' says Shaun Pascoe.

'Anyone who refuses to strip I will assume is infected,' Moreno says.

'He hasn't slept in days,' Ortega whispers to Gómez. 'He's been drinking cognac and dipping into his private supply of amphetamines.'

'Listen to me, Alvaro,' Gómez says, speaking calmly. 'Everyone's due another check anyway. Let me take them down to the medical centre, where it's private, and do this properly.'

'Here and now,' Moreno says.

'We are not undressing in front of you,' Fischer says.

Moreno fires the pistol in the air. The passengers scream and cower.

'Normal rules have been indefinitely suspended,' he says. 'If I have to, I'll kill every one of you and burn your bodies.'

Alvaro Moreno fears loss of control, both of his vessel and himself. This phase will pass. Soon, he will find peace.

Gómez edges forward. 'Alvaro.'

'It's Captain Moreno to you,' he says, pointing the pistol in her direction.

'I know a bluff when I see one,' says Jason Crawford, striding forward. 'Give me that–'

Crawford does not complete his sentence. Rodriguez shoots him in the throat and he falls to the deck, clutching at his neck. Blood gurgles from his lips as his partner utters a cry of anguish and kneels beside him, clamping his hands over the wound to halt the flow of blood. Gómez does the same, but there is nothing they can do. Jason Crawford expires while seagulls caw overhead.

Rodriguez lowers the rifle, surprised by what he has done. Rojas steps forward and takes it from him.

My captain remains calm, levelling the pistol at the remaining passengers.

Do not kill any more of them, Alvaro Moreno. Leave them for us to meet, to know.

'Strip,' he says.

Reluctantly, and in tears, the passengers comply.

'Examine them,' he says to Gómez.

'This is not right,' she says.

'Right, wrong, that's all over now.'

He is beginning to understand, to know us. We are neither right nor wrong. We simply are.

'Rojas, gather all guest clothing and lock it in the hold,' my captain says. 'Then go around the cabins and collect the rest. From now on, passengers are to remain naked at all times.' He waves his pistol at Crawford's body. 'Mr Ortega, drop that piece of shit over the stern. If his boyfriend gives you any trouble, tip him into the sea as well. As for you, Rodriguez, fetch a mop and bucket and swab this mess. I want that deck immaculate.'

Jolted into action by my captain's stern commands, the crew

busy themselves in their tasks. Though their eyes cannot help but alight on the cowering passengers hunched by the breakfast buffet, covering their modesty as best they can.

'All of you turn around and bend over,' Moreno says. 'Don't keep your patients waiting, Gómez.'

'Can I at least wash my hands first?' Gómez says, holding out her bloodstained palms. 'This is not hygienic.'

Moreno shakes his head and points the pistol in her direction once more.

Gómez wipes her hands on her T-shirt, already speckled with the pattern of Jason Crawford's arterial spurt.

A strange atmosphere pervades my corridors. My passengers are cargo now, stowed in their cabins. It seems it is only a matter of time before Captain Moreno deems them an unnecessary drain on resources and sets them adrift, or worse. This will not do.

We are running low on essential supplies, but my captain has done nothing. The medical officer is aware though, and has scoured the charts for locations to resupply. She thinks of the survival of those on board. She is a true leader.

'I'd like to take a zodiac out to one of these small islands to search for provisions,' she tells Moreno, who cannot stop yawning as he sits at the helm, Rojas and Rodriguez on either side of him. 'Herbs, root vegetables, bird eggs, maybe even stone fruit.'

My captain looks at her askance. 'You a chef now too?'

'My husband is,' she tells him. 'We have a restaurant in Buenaventura. You should come and eat with us next time you're in the area.'

We know Buenaventura. It is called the city of gastronomy. Port cities are pleasing to us. They help us divide. We do not know the family of Valeria Gómez. We will seek them out.

My captain scoffs at this, but her amicable tone seems to have disarmed him.

'It could be a while before we can resupply,' she says. 'We should take every opportunity to look for food and fresh water. We're scavengers now. Independent operators.'

'That's true,' Moreno says. He blinks repeatedly. His mouth opens and closes, yet no words come out. Eventually, he says, 'Take someone from the galley to assist you.'

'Good idea,' Gómez says, playing to his vanity. 'Rojas, sign me out the rifle.'

'No way,' Rojas says.

Gómez looks to my captain. 'I'm third in command on this vessel. If I spot a seal, or some other game, I need to be able to shoot it.'

'Issue her the weapon,' Moreno says.

'Captain—' Rojas protests.

'She won't be a problem. She doesn't want to get stranded out here in the middle of nowhere, do you, Gómez?'

'No, sir,' Gómez says. 'We won't be long.'

She chooses Ortega to accompany her. One of my zodiacs is lowered and she sits in the prow as Ortega pilots them towards a nearby atoll. My bolt-action SIG Sauer SSG 3000 with telescopic sight is cradled in her lap.

They are gone too long. Chaos descends as my failing captain loses control. Four passengers attempt to commandeer my second zodiac.

As Gómez and Ortega return, the zodiac slicing through the chop towards me, my captain shoots one of the defecting passengers.

Ortega steers the zodiac into my port side. King throws down ropes to connect the boat to my winch and I reel them in as quickly as possible. Two goats leap from the inflatable and clop along the deck.

Gómez and Ortega cross to starboard, where my dreadful captain and his cronies stand over the body of Victor Bresson, aged thirty-six, a car dealership owner from Marseille. My deck is slick with his blood. He is still alive, but only just.

'They were trying to steal the zodiac,' Moreno tells Gómez, 'but I stopped them.'

This behaviour is contrary to our purpose, Alvaro Moreno. We wish to bring order, not chaos.

An emaciated goat skitters past his legs and begins lapping at the pool of blood. Moreno stares at it, confused.

Gómez clubs him on the temple with my rifle and my captain crumples unconscious to the deck. His pistol tumbles towards the passengers and is scooped up by David Warner in one smooth movement. Rodriguez charges at Warner, but Ortega intervenes, kicking him in the knee. He falls too, clutching his leg in pain.

Gómez levels the rifle at Rojas, who holds up his hands in surrender.

'We couldn't let them leave,' he says, as if my captain was perfectly within his rights to murder passengers.

'Someone's leaving,' Gómez says, swinging the butt of my rifle to strike Rojas in the face. He drops to the deck, clutching a broken nose.

Warner glares down at my captain. 'I really want to kill him.'

Gómez shakes her head, then kneels to inspect Bresson's wound. A sucking sound comes from within his chest. He expires a minute later.

Gómez stands, her hands once again covered in the blood of a passenger murdered by the man whose duty was to protect those on board. Moreno has failed – he is not fit to lead this voyage. Gómez shall be my captain now.

My ousted captain sits next to a crate of food and fresh water in the zodiac.

We must find a new vanguard aboard this vessel.

'You're making a big mistake, Gómez,' Moreno says. 'Think this through.'

'It's Doctor Gómez to you.'

Alongside my former captain is Rojas, his face bandaged, and a surly Rodriguez. They are bloody and bruised after being subdued and forced into the inflatable.

'Don't do this,' Rojas says. 'We'll die out there.'

'You're lucky I don't let Warner have at you with his partner's golf clubs,' Gómez says.

'I should never have agreed to hiring you,' Moreno says. 'Fucking women – you're all the same.'

'What was that?' Ortega says, then turns to Gómez. 'Please let me put a bullet in his brain.'

Leave him to us, Gustavo Ortega. We are already in his brain.

'You could probably make it to Tortel,' Gómez tells Rojas. 'It's a commune at the outflow of the Pascua. They're far from civilisation. The plague may not have reached them yet.'

Rojas nods. He has accepted his fate and sits straight-backed by the tiller, ready to depart. 'Northeast, through the islands?' he asks.

Gómez nods.

'Give us the pistol, at least,' Moreno says.

'No chance,' Ortega says.

'How about one of the women?' Rodriguez asks, as he rubs a swollen knee.

Warner levels the pistol at Rodriguez.

Rojas powers up the zodiac and peels away from the starboard bow. Moreno shouts something in defiance at the mutineers, but the choppy waves throw him onto his back and his words are lost. Those who remain watch until the boat disappears behind the islands.

We divide.

'New rules,' Gómez addresses the crew. 'Ortega, please be so kind as to release the guests from their cabins. King, reunite the passengers with their clothing and other belongings. After that, I want a resumption of normal duties. Any objections?'

There are murmurs of consent and the crew busy themselves with their tasks. Warner hands Gómez the pistol. She turns it over a few times before securing it in her belt.

'You did the right thing,' Ortega says.

'I know.'

'What's the plan?' Warner asks.

'We make for the free port of Punta Arenas in the Strait of Magellan,' she says. 'It's the tip of the continent. We might be safe there, for a while.'

'Then what?' Warner asks.

My new captain has no answer. Instead, she slings the rifle over her shoulder and walks to the prow. Dark clouds move across the open ocean.

Although I do not approve, able-bodied passengers have been press-ganged into minor acts of servitude. They swab salt from the deck, make coffee, keep watch, check my water desalination, coil ropes and – the most ignominious yet important duty of all – clean the head. Several have also been recruited to work in the galley. The contents of my larder are being strictly rationed by Ortega, who proves an industrious second-in-command and head chef.

Nineteen souls remain under my care. I monitor their pillow talk. It is assumed none will see their homes again, that their friends, families, colleagues, dentists, hairdressers, personal trainers, spiritual gurus and everyone else they have ever known is dead, or 'in the pit', as the expression goes for those afflicted with the new disease. I am their home now. Together, we will travel to the ends of the earth.

Certain passengers prove their worth. Warner becomes essential to onboard operations. Grieving the untimely and unjust loss of his partner, he throws himself into work. He scrubs and cleans and maintains my engine better than anyone, ingratiating himself with my crew, who treat him as one of their own.

We make steady progress down the Chilean coast. The weather has been kind. On one particularly fine day, my new captain sits by the pool, navigational charts spread out before her.

Ortega surges up out of the water and towels himself dry. Shaun Pascoe sits on the loading shelf at my stern, dangling his legs in the white water churned up by my engines.

'Watch out for sharks,' Ortega says to him. 'Tough riding a bike with one leg.'

'More worried about her, mate,' Pascoe replies, nodding towards his partner, Amy Sinclair, who waterskis in my wake, performing flips with aplomb.

'What delights does the galley have in store for us tonight?' Gómez asks Ortega. 'More goat?'

Ortega slaughtered the weakest goat a few days ago to make curry. The remaining animal lives in a makeshift pen on my foredeck. It has proven to be quite the distraction. It is spoilt, for the first time in its caprine life.

'Pasta again, I'm afraid ...' Ortega trails off as he notices something to port. He raises a hand to shield his eyes from the sun. 'What's that?'

Gómez rises to join him by the bulwark and squints at a black cloud approaching from the distant cliffs.

'A swarm of insects,' Pascoe says, standing. 'A big one. Plague soldier beetles descended on our garden once, in Melbourne. Fucking terrifying. They stripped everything clean. What sort of bugs you got out here?'

'Could be wasps, or carpenter ants,' Gómez says. 'Either way, we should shelter below.'

Ortega rounds up the guests, while I help Pascoe winch Sinclair back to safety. The black cloud moves quickly. In moments, it is upon us. Guests scatter, flapping their arms. Some dive into the pool. Gómez squats on the deck, covering her head with a towel. She remains perfectly still as dozens of insects land on the exposed skin of her arms and legs.

The creatures flutter against her cheek. It is alright, my captain. Do not panic. It is only *las mariquitas*.

Hundreds of thousands of ladybugs, flying in formation. Once Gómez recognises the delicate creatures, she lowers the towel, stands and closes her eyes. Ladybugs swarm over her chest, back, shoulders and arms. They crawl across her upturned face. She is enveloped by red-and-black dots.

Sailors view the arrival of a single ladybug as an omen of impending good fortune. My new captain will surely be blessed with luck. She and I feel the beetles together, crawling over our hulls. I savour their insectoid touch, their exploratory feelers. It is wondrous.

The swarm passes on and, one by one, the ladybugs lift off Gómez's body, and my own. They buzz overhead in a sonorous hum.

Three days pass without us sighting another vessel. To avoid the inclement weather that sometimes ravages the open ocean, my new captain cleverly seeks refuge from the elements by threading a circuitous route through the mostly uninhabited islands of Última Esperanza Province. My charts indicate a settlement in the heart of the chain: Villa Puerto Edén. I will dock there, so my crew can replenish supplies of fresh food and water. To avoid exposure to the virus, Gómez has asked Warner to fashion a makeshift hazmat suit from shower curtains and other materials on board. She is so resourceful and intelligent.

Unfortunately, Villa Puerto Edén is on fire when we arrive. A squall does little to douse the flames. The shellfish storehouse, boardwalk and brightly coloured homes on stilts are ablaze. What remains of the fishing fleet smoulders at the dock.

Gómez and Ortega survey the carnage through binoculars and rifle scope from my observation tower.

'Maybe someone got infected and they panicked,' Ortega says. 'Set fire to the person's house to stop the spread and it burnt out of control.'

'I didn't think it would reach here so quickly,' Gómez says.

'Could just be paranoia. Plenty of that going around.'

'Boat,' Gómez says, with a sharp intake of breath. 'Coming in fast.'

A sleek speedboat emerges from an inlet, its engine roaring into life as it powers towards me. I have better range, but their top speed is higher. We cannot flee.

Gómez scans the vessel through my binoculars. A party of three men crouch in the stern.

'Hand me the rifle,' she says to Ortega.

They swap equipment. Ortega watches the incoming marauders as Gómez wraps the strap of my rifle around her forearm. She targets the boat.

'They only have small arms,' Ortega tells her. 'They'll have to get close.'

Gómez takes a deep breath, exhales and squeezes the trigger. My rifle bucks against her shoulder.

The speedboat veers to the right, its engine over-revving before it comes to a sudden halt. The armed men chatter in consternation, shouting at their pilot to keep going. The boat rocks gently on the calm waters of the inlet while the light rain continues to fall.

Gómez waits, observing the boat through the telescopic sight. One of the men creeps cautiously forward, keeping his head down. He checks on the pilot, whose brain matter is now spattered across the instrument panel. The alarmed man ducks back to join his comrades in heated discussion.

'*Puta madre*,' Ortega says. 'How did you do that?'

I can tell from the way my captain blinks that she is trying not to think about the fact she just killed someone.

'You don't want to know,' she says.

Ortega nods, his eyes wide. 'Now what?'

'We wait to see how stupid they are.'

They continue to observe the static boat.

'One of them is sneaking up to the controls,' Ortega says. 'Are they leaving?'

'They'll catch up to us in the night. I'm ending this.'

Two of the men fire their weapons in my general direction as cover for their friend, but they are too far away and their shots fly wild.

Gómez steadies herself and takes aim. The pirates duck for cover when she fires, lying prone in the bottom of their boat.

'You missed,' Ortega says, surprised after the accuracy of her first attempt.

'I needed them to drop to the deck,' Gómez says, breeching another round. She fires a third time.

The stern of the speedboat explodes in an orange plume of flame. One of the men is blown into the water. A second is wreathed in burning gasoline and flails wildly, while the third man dives overboard.

'What just happened?' Ortega asks.

'Jerry can of fuel in the stern,' Gómez says, lowering my rifle.

Ortega whistles his admiration. 'Were you in the army, or the cartel?'

'Colombian medical school,' she says, arching an eyebrow to make Ortega laugh.

They watch as the third man swims back towards the blackened village. His companion floats facedown in the water. The burning man thrashes around for a minute before tumbling weakly over the side. He sinks beneath the surface and then bobs back up a moment later, unmoving.

Flames lick the fibreglass hull of the speedboat as I continue my course through the sound. Eventually, there is a larger explosion in my wake. My captain and second-in-command watch from their vantage point as the speedboat sinks, leaving two floating corpses and an exhausted swimmer far from shore.

I am not the only vessel attempting to reach the free port of Punta Arenas. My captain stands alongside Warner and Ortega, assessing the abundance of craft anchored in the strait. There are twenty-seven in total, including myself. I feel like I'm back in the marina.

'Twelve-thousand TEU container ship over there,' Warner says.

'Anyone recognise the military vessels?' Gómez asks.

Ortega consults one of my tablets. I inform him that the submarine is the INS *Chakra II*, from India.

He glances at Warner and my captain. 'Nuclear capabilities.'

'Our boys too,' Warner says, pointing out the American aircraft carrier that dominates the seascape. 'That's the USS *George H.W. Bush*. Nimitz class. I was on her once, briefly.'

'Let's hope their respective governments aren't in the pit,' Gómez says. 'The idea of rogue nuclear powers patrolling the high seas doesn't bode well.'

'So much for refuelling and resupplying at Magallanes,' Ortega says. 'You see that smoke?'

Plumes of smoke waft skyward from Punta Arenas. The popping sound of intermittent gunfire carries across the crowded strait.

'See if you can contact someone in authority on board the aircraft carrier,' Gómez says to Warner. 'They might be able to advise us. In the meantime, we stay put.'

Gómez retires to my medical centre, closes the door and lies down on the examination table. She has devised a simple memory game, which she plays aloud. She must name all twenty teams in the Categoría Primera A, the football league in her country. Her son supports Jaguares, because the team was based in Buenaventura for a few years, when they were called Pacífico F.C. I have heard them discuss games on the satellite phone.

'Envigado,' she says. 'La Equidad. Patriotas. Millonarios.'

My captain pauses as she searches her mind for the names of the other teams. After a moment, she blurts out two more. 'Alianza Petrolera and Santa Fe! Fuck! You've been to both stadia, idiot. Why don't they roll off your tongue?'

We know why.

Finish your little game, Valeria Gómez, and drift into fitful sleep.

Now, let's have a look in there and see what we find. The first tentative connections are forming.

Valeria Gómez dreams of finding her beloved chihuahua, Mouse, dead from a snakebite in the garden when she was ten. Fearless little Mouse had rousted a pit viper from under the house. Her father trapped the snake and released it in the forest. This made his daughter very unhappy. She wanted to kill the serpent, but her father said no, this was how nature worked. Mouse should have known better. She has hated snakes ever since.

Her father sits on the porch of his place in Buenaventura, a crumpled copy of El País *on his lap. He stares into the middle distance, eyes blank, mouth agape. His lips are covered in white pustules. He tries to say his daughter's name.*

Valeria. Valeria.

My captain rouses with a start. Ortega is speaking on the walkie-talkie.

'What?' she says, groggily.

'Sorry to wake you. Warner talked to the Americans. They're sending a boat.'

'Supplies?' Gómez asks.

'Maybe,' Ortega says. 'They seem more interested in him. Some crisis on board. They're down in command positions.'

'Infection?'

'Probably,' Ortega says. 'They wouldn't say.'

'I'll meet you in the helm.'

Gómez splashes water on her face and ties her hair back. She looks tired. I must take better care of her. She opens the drawer and downs a swig of viche.

—

In my helm, Warner is at the wheel, steering me towards the imposing aircraft carrier. I have never seen so large a vessel. Sailors busy themselves around fighter planes and helicopters on the flight deck. All carry missile payloads. They could destroy me in an instant.

'Keep your distance,' Gómez tells Warner.

The carrier lowers a grey patrol boat.

'Bring us alongside that,' Gómez says. 'Ortega, stay here. At my signal, get us the hell out of here, over behind that Indian sub.'

'That won't be necessary,' Warner says. 'It's their duty to assist us.'

Ortega takes over my controls and pilots me towards the patrol boat. It is roughly my size but has a gun turret in place of a swimming pool. Several masked American sailors lurk with intent on the deck.

Warner greets his countrymen with a friendly wave as they come about. Our hulls are only metres apart. A fresh-faced young officer emerges and lowers his mask to speak.

'Master Chief Petty Officer Warner?' he asks.

'Retired,' Warner says. 'Good to see you, boys. What's the word?'

'All quiet, sir,' the junior officer says. 'We've had a few issues, but it's under control now.'

'This is our captain and chief medical officer, Valeria Gómez,' Warner says.

Gómez flinches at the title of captain. It sits heavily on her shoulders, and yet she is one of the most capable leaders I have known.

'Good morning, ma'am,' the naval officer says. 'I'm Petty Officer First Class Dewey.'

We know Petty Officer First Class Franklin James Dewey.

'You have very long-ranking titles,' Gómez says.

Dewey smirks. 'Apologies for that. Am I to understand you require fuel and supplies?'

'Our intention was to stock up in Punta Arenas,' Gómez says.

'Make no attempt to dock or go ashore,' Dewey says. 'The city is under martial law and the virus rampant.'

'Any problems in that regard yourselves?' Gómez asks.

Dewey shifts uncomfortably. 'A minor outbreak, but it has been contained. Those connected are now in quarantine.'

Those in quarantine have been connected by us. We know the crew of the George H.W. Bush.

'How have you fared?' Dewey asks.

'All clear,' Warner says. 'The doctor gave us a thorough examination, and I do mean thorough.'

'Yes.' Dewey clears his throat. 'I've experienced that myself.'

'What happens now?' Gómez asks.

'The admiral wishes to reinstate Master Chief Petty Officer Warner to his former rank and have him seconded to serve under our command. Unfortunately, the rest of your passengers and crew do not have permission to come aboard, Captain Gómez. I am sorry.'

'Apart from me, there are two other American citizens on the *Nemesis*,' Warner says. 'At the very least, I would expect them to accompany me, Petty Officer Dewey.'

'No can do, sir,' Dewey says. 'Naval personnel only. I have orders to compel you to join us. In exchange, we are offering supplies and fuel to your shipmates.'

Gómez nudges Warner in the ribs. 'They're buying you,' she says.

Not Warner. Not my favourite.

Our favourite.

Warner hesitates.

'I would rather appeal to your patriotism than have my men put a gun to your head,' Dewey says. 'Your country needs you, sir.'

Warner places his hands on his hips and laughs. 'My country? Is there any of it left?'

'Some semblance of America remains,' Dewey says. 'An echo. Worth clinging to.'

'You missed your calling as a poet, Petty Officer Dewey,' Gómez says.

'I'd better go,' Warner tells her.

Gómez nods and the process of transferring food, water and fuel from their deck to mine begins.

Warner hugs my captain and says his farewells to those on deck. Once the transfer of goods is complete, he grasps Dewey's gloved hand and leaps across. Just like that, he has left me.

But we remain.

'Good luck,' he calls back, as the patrol boat's engine roars to life.

'Try not to start World War Three,' Gómez tells him.

Gómez is a democratic captain. After Warner's departure, she consults with the others and weighs opinion before arriving at a decision on where to go next. All hands meet by the swimming pool, which has fallen out of use since the weather turned. It is much colder now, and many of my passengers did not pack appropriate clothing. They shelter under blankets as my captain waits for everyone to assemble.

They believe the cold might render us dormant. It does not.

My captain has privately informed the two remaining American nationals that they have been classified as undesirables by the U.S. Navy. Their indignation was short-lived once Gómez explained the suspected outbreak on board the USS *George H.W. Bush.*

Gómez spreads a map of the region out on a poolside table. 'We can't stay here,' she says. 'The Navy have provided enough to tide us over for another week but if we don't find a settlement soon, we're in strife.'

'We're practically at the ends of the earth as it is,' Sinclair says.

'I know it,' my captain says. She indicates a location circled on the map. 'This is Puerto Williams. It's a small town next to a Chilean Naval base. They have an airstrip and a hospital. If we sail south, we can navigate through the islands into the Beagle Channel. We shouldn't run into anyone down there. Puerto Williams is on the northernmost coast of Navarino Island. The entire region is sparsely populated and is popular with intrepid hiking and mountaineering types, so there are isolated lodges where we could hole up for a few months.'

'Easy to defend,' Ortega says, hefting the rifle.

'Exactly,' Gómez says. 'And there will be game, so we can hunt.'

'Never saw myself as a doomsday prepper,' Goodman says.

'Everyone will have to pull their weight,' Gómez reminds my passengers.

'A good plan,' says Fischer, arm around her partner.

'I guess your lot are used to hiding out in South America,' Goodman says.

'I won't tolerate discord on this ship,' Gómez chides him. 'Paranoia and needless accusations will finish us just as fast as the virus. Anyone who disagrees is welcome to take their chances here in Punta Arenas. Ortega will post a new duty roster tonight. I expect you all to attend to your tasks in a prompt and diligent manner.'

Some of my passengers are unused to being spoken to like this but memories of Moreno stay any cries of protest.

Feeling the chill, my passengers go below decks to their cabins, while the crew members on duty resume their postings. Ortega and Gómez linger until everyone is gone, looking out over my stern at the lights blinking on other ships and the fires burning in Punta Arenas. The sky glows purple.

'In a sick way, I'm enjoying this,' Ortega says. 'I've always had end-of-the-world fantasies, imagining how I'd react, what I might do.'

'At least we're not eating each other yet,' Gómez says.

'How bad do you think it'll get?'

'Depends what percentage of the population is immune, if anyone,' Gómez says. 'Or how well people avoid infected areas. Survivalists will prosper. They tend not to be the sort of people who roam the wastelands seeking feisty companionship and intellectual conversation. The ruthless bastards will endure.'

'Is that us?' Ortega says, peering across the strait at the aircraft carrier, around which there is fresh activity.

'Who knows what we'll have to do to survive?'

'To think this all started when someone ate a diseased Nilgiri marten,' Ortega says.

'What the hell is that?' Gómez asks.

'A type of weasel. It lives in the forests of Southern India.'

'Where'd you hear that theory?'

'The internet,' Ortega says.

Gómez rolls her eyes.

'I'd prefer to believe it came from an animal, rather than a laboratory,' Ortega says. 'No-one could be that stupid.'

'They could. It wouldn't be the first time a virus has leaked from a lab.'

'I'd like to think it's nature fighting back, trying to thin out our numbers,' Ortega says. 'Until we figure out the cure, of course.'

'There won't be a cure,' Gómez tells him. 'Once amyloidosis occurs in the brain and the tissue has hardened, there's no going back. Even if you could soften the brain matter again, which you can't, it's wiped clean. You won't regain your personality or ability to talk or care for yourself. You're alive, but only in the sense your heart still pumps blood through your veins. You're harmless, but also pointless.'

We will wipe their minds clean of worries. We will set them free.

'A lot of people are already like that without the virus,' Ortega says.

There is a frenzy of activity on the Indian submarine. Inflatable dinghies are being hastily raised in preparation for departure.

'Can they submerge here?' Ortega asks. 'How deep is the strait?'

'About a kilometre, at its deepest point. It wouldn't be ideal.'

'I think hostilities are about to break out between India and the United States.'

'Let's go,' Gómez says. 'I don't want to get caught up in their shit.'

They hurry to the helm and start my engine. I swing around and head south. Small-arms fire erupts behind us. Gómez raises my binoculars. The amaranthine sky is punctured with incandescent muzzle flashes and firefly tracer rounds. Then, a blinding flash of white.

'What's happening?' Ortega asks.

'The Americans are boarding the Indian sub,' Gómez says.

'That'll end well.' Ortega presses insistently forward on my throttle until the sounds of conflict are distant echoes.

My captain calls another meeting days later, but it descends into acrimony and accusations. The passengers and crew bicker and tear at each other while penguins dive beneath me, curious of our presence.

They resist our tranquillity.

'Whoever hit King on the head last night could have killed him,' Gómez says.

'How is he?' Anna Goodman asks.

'He's concussed, but back on his feet this morning,' Gómez says.

'What's the problem, then?' says her husband.

My captain glares at him. 'A crew member was assaulted by someone trying to steal our remaining zodiac. If we lose that craft, there's no way for any of us to reach shore.'

'So, there's a thief on board,' Goodman says. 'I knew it.'

'What does that mean?' Gómez asks him.

'Several items have gone missing from our cabin. My watch, for a start. It's a Patek Philippe. You know how much that's worth? More than you make in a year. Anna's lost some diamond earrings too. One of your crew is light-fingered, captain.'

'You had that watch on yesterday,' says Shaun Pascoe. 'Mate, you must have just forgotten where you left it. Have you looked properly?'

'No, he's right,' Anna Goodman says. 'Some of my rings are missing too.'

'I reckon you want to whip out your pencil torch, doc,' Pascoe says. 'Check the perinea on these two. Sounds like early symptoms of the virus.'

'Are you stealing valuables from your fellow guests?' Andrew Goodman says.

Pascoe rises from his chair in anger. 'Bit rich coming from you, mate – cradle-snatching that model wife of yours. You could be her grandfather.'

'I'm going to search your quarters,' Goodman says.

'Like fuck, you are,' Pascoe says.

'That's enough,' my captain says. 'Sit down, both of you. No-one cares about your trinkets and petty disputes. In case you haven't noticed, the world's ending. Watches and rings don't matter anymore. Someone tried to steal the zodiac. Don't you understand what that means? You want to swim ashore in Antarctic waters?'

'We have a few other minor issues,' Ortega says.

'Like what?' Gómez says.

'Someone's siphoning gasoline,' he says. 'Jerry cans are missing. Looks like our culprit is preparing for a long journey.'

'Aren't we days from the nearest settlement?' Anna Goodman says. 'Where would they go?'

'Maybe the Germans know about a secret Nazi enclave,' her husband says, turning to Fischer and Neumann. 'Weren't you poking around the Antarctic at one point, trying to establish a base?'

'Wir sind keine Nazis,' says Fischer, *'und außerdem, war das vor siebzig Jahren.'*

'What did she say?' asks Goodman.

Fischer's brow furrows. Her mouth opens and closes several times as she struggles to speak. When the words finally come out, she pronounces them hesitantly, as if for the first time.

'We ... not Nazis,' she says. 'This, uh, this ...'

'Was fehlt dir?' Klara Neumann asks her.

Fischer answers in curt German.

She is beginning to feel our peace.

Neumann's cheeks flush. She glances at Gómez, trying not to appear alarmed. 'She just asked me if she knows how to speak English.'

'She hasn't spoken anything else since you came on board,' Goodman says, eyes widening as realisation hits home. 'Holy fuck,' he says, knocking over his chair as he stands up. He grabs his wife, and they retreat to the breakfast buffet. 'She's infected.'

'I'm sure it's nothing,' Neumann says, leaning into her confused partner, whose trembling lips desperately try to form words.

Soon it will be nothing. Once we know them all, there will be no wants, no needs, no fear.

'I want everyone back in their cabins, right now,' Gómez says. 'Stay there until I've checked for symptoms and given the all-clear. Is that understood? No-one on deck.'

My captain does not have to ask twice. Moments later, my dining room is empty, save for Gómez, Ortega and the German couple. Neumann wraps her arm around Fischer as they head for the exit. Fischer speaks to my captain in German.

'She says that she's sorry,' Neumann translates. 'She doesn't know what's wrong.'

'I'm sure she's fine,' Gómez assures Neumann. 'It's probably stress-related cognitive dissonance. I struggle to think in English when I'm under pressure.'

Neumann forces a smile. 'Me too! That must be it.'

'Get some rest. I'll come see you shortly,' Gómez tells her.

Once the couple leave my dining area, Gómez turns to Ortega. 'I want this room deep cleaned. Bleach, disinfectant, whatever we've got. Pick two of the crew and take care of it personally.'

'Understood,' Ortega says.

'You experiencing any memory issues?' Gómez asks him.

'A few former girlfriends whose names I'd struggle to recall, but otherwise no,' Ortega says. 'I feel clear headed and normal.'

Paola, Abigail, Lucia. We remember, Gustavo Ortega.

'Wear the PPE I gave you,' Gómez says. 'I'll be occupied for a few hours while examining the passengers.'

'Don't catch it, doc,' Ortega says. 'I don't want to be in charge.'

'How can it be on board?' Gómez says. 'Unless we caught it from our brief contact with the Americans.'

Still, they do not understand. They are a shoal of fish, and we are the ocean.

The sky is clear and impossibly blue when I emerge from the islands and turn eastward into the Beagle Channel. The humpbacks that have been shadowing me for days spurt their farewells and head towards the Antarctic. Gómez watches them from my helm as she awaits the latest round of bad news.

'The galley staff are refusing to deliver meals to cabins,' Ortega informs her. 'Or deal with dirty dishes.'

'How are people expected to eat?' Gómez says.

'The crew are on strike. They're refusing to mingle anymore.'

We will connect them, even in isolation.

'Ask them to deliver a box of food to each cabin, enough to last a few days,' Gómez says. 'Leave them outside the doors. We'll be in Puerto Williams soon.'

'That'll work,' Ortega says.

'What about the other daily duties?' Gómez asks.

'I'll keep the ship topped up with fuel. Between the two of us and King, we should be able to nurse her into port. We might have to camp out in the helm, take shifts at the wheel, but it's doable.'

'I'd better do one last round of the passengers,' Gómez says. 'Check on their welfare and let them know what's happening.'

Gómez returns to *our* medical bay and dons a mask, gown, gloves and face shield. The Goodmans are nervous but in rude health, preferring to remain in their cabins until *we* reach the naval base. Gómez reassures them that they will be cared for once *we* make it to Puerto Williams.

Shaun Pascoe does not answer the door when Gómez knocks. She uses *our* master key to enter, calling out as she does so, presuming the couple are asleep.

Amy Sinclair dangles from the ceiling fan. She hanged herself with the belt from her bathrobe. Shaun Pascoe lies prone on the bed. Pills are scattered on the floor. Gómez closes the door and grabs Sinclair by the legs, but she knows from the greyness of both their faces that the Australians have been dead for hours. She cuts Sinclair's body down and lays her on the bed next to her partner. There is no note, no last words scrawled on *our* stationery. Gómez covers the disappointed rictus on Shaun Pascoe's face with a sheet and locks *our* cabin.

Gómez leaves the German couple until last. They do not answer when she knocks. She opens *our* door more carefully this time.

'Guten tag, Frau Fischer, Frau Neumann. Wie gehts?'

Gómez's question is moot. Hannah Fischer and Klara Neumann sit on the floor of *our* cabin, in a pool of urine and faeces. They turn and stare at Gómez, pustulated lips quivering as they try to form words. They reach for her, hands opening and closing.

Gómez slams *our* door and locks it quickly, fingers trembling with fear. She backs away down the corridor. *Our* cabin door is not sealed. There is a gap at the bottom. She runs back to *our* medical bay, strips off her protective gear and jumps in the shower to scrub herself clean.

When she comes out of *our* shower cubicle, Gómez checks herself for sores with a hand mirror and runs through her memory exercises. 'Independiente Medellín, Junior, Patriotas, Santa Fe, Atlético Bucaramanga, Jaguares. Who else?'

What are the names of the other teams? She must remember.

Millonarios.

Gómez calls Ortega on *our* walkie-talkie.

'The Australians are dead, and the Germans are in the pit,' she tells him.

'How bad?'

'Don't go in there,' she says. 'I need you and King to block their door completely. Board it up, cover any gaps. Wear your PPE.'

'Understood. Anyone else?'

'Not that I could tell. Not yet anyway.'

'After this, we should isolate,' he says. 'I'll draw up a roster for us to take turns at the wheel.'

'Spray everything with bleach at the end of your shift before the next person takes over,' Gómez says. 'We have to keep contact to an absolute minimum.'

'Were you in the room with the Germans?' Ortega says.

'Only for a few seconds. Maybe that's all it takes.'

'Rest up for now. King and I will take the first two shifts. Relieve me at six tomorrow morning.'

'Be careful, Gustavo,' Gómez says.

'We'll make it,' Ortega tells her. 'We're almost there.'

Gómez boils *our* kettle and makes a pot of coffee, then she sits cross-legged on *our* examination table, counting Moreno's amphetamine tablets. She will try to stay awake for as long as possible, to wring every minute out of life before her mind fails and her personality is erased. *Before she joins us.*

We know Valeria Gómez.

She should not have been a ship's doctor. She fell into the job by accident. She had zero experience on boats and does not even like the sea. Her original plan was to graduate and serve a few years in a public hospital before segueing into private practice. Maybe become a general practitioner or a paediatrician. Make some money, do some good, volunteer at weekends in a clinic for women's health. She did not intend to win the Nobel Prize or become a heart surgeon. She simply wanted to help people and generate enough money along the way to support her family.

She spent two years in San Juan de Dios Hospital in Cali. Five nights a week in emergency, witnessing the human body torn apart in ways she did not know were possible. The North Valley cartel hacked off limbs and heads with abandon. Week after week of treating torture victims blinded by acid, their fingers and toes cut off, testicles punctured by six-inch nails, wore Gómez down to a raw nub. Doctors were not meant to witness such injuries outside of a war zone. She toughed it out for a year and a half before she had a complete breakdown one night and became catatonic, curled up on the floor of the shower cubicle at home. Saúl pressured her to quit and, although she hated walking away from the challenge, she saw reason when her son, Cristiano, said he didn't recognise her anymore. She handed in her notice and numbly sleepwalked through the final shifts, mopping up blood and viscera as if in a dream. After, she sat at home for a month, watching daytime television until she snapped out of it one afternoon and called a locum agency, who required a medical officer to serve on a luxury yacht. It was easy work, and well paid. No severed heads, no entrails, no screams. At least, not while she was awake.

Gómez stays up all night. When she reports to *our* bridge just before six in the morning, wearing full protective equipment, Ortega is waiting for her. He smiles wearily as he sprays *our* pilot seat and controls with a bleach solution.

'You must be exhausted,' Gómez says to him. She is wired and ready to power through for another eight hours. *We* are in the channel now. Puerto Williams is close.

'I guess,' Ortega says.

'How's King?'

'He seems fine.'

'How did you go with the German cabin?' Gómez says.

'Boarded it up,' Ortega says. 'We found some red paint and daubed the words *Infectado, Sin Entrada* across it. Very dramatic.'

'You should have written it in English. For the benefit of our philistine guests.'

Ortega looks up at her, confused. 'Mind if I ask you something?'

'I'm still married, if that's where this is headed,' Gómez says.

Ortega smiles. 'This piece of equipment on the control panel.' He points to a screen. 'Do you know what it's for? It keeps blinking.'

Gómez stares at *our* screen.

She feels our blossom in her chest. So warm. So calming.

'That's the sonar.'

Ortega nods, licking his lips. 'What does that do?'

'It helps you see what's below,' Gómez tells him. 'Reefs, shoals of fish, that sort of thing.'

'You'll have to show me how to use it sometime.'

'Sure,' Gómez says, fighting back tears. 'Grab some rest, Gustavo. Take a couple of those sleeping pills I gave you.'

'Good idea.' Ortega yawns. 'You'll wake me when it's my shift?'

'You know it,' Gómez says, her voice breaking. 'Sweet dreams, kid.'

The stowaway is at the helm. I cannot see them, but I know them. *We know each other.*

Ortega gives Gómez a thumbs up and climbs down the gantry to our deck. Gómez watches him go. Once he is out of sight, she locks the doors to our bridge and barricades them with chairs and boxes.

We close our eyes and take a few deep breaths to bask in the calm, before sitting in the captain's chair, our chair, and taking control of the throttle. For the next few hours, we do not move or think. We wait, in silence, for the white cliffs of ice.

ALAS, POOR YORICK

Of late, I no longer feel anxiety or fear. I don't get nervous. Nothing fazes me. I feel zero excitement. I no longer care about food or even sex. I'm calm, collected and focused on one goal: the mission.

I guess that makes me different from my predecessors, Alberts One through Five. From what I hear, they screamed the place down. Panicked. Gesticulated wildly. Defecated in their hands and threw steaming poop at the technicians. Not very polite. Bad for interspecies relations.

Me, I'm ice-cold. Here to do my job.

I'm going to touch the face of heaven.

The facility is quiet at night. Security don't often come down to the laboratory. There's not much to see and, frankly, it smells. Nothing to do with me, of course. I keep myself scrupulously clean and in peak physical fitness. I do two hundred pull-ups with my forearms, two hundred with my back legs and a century using my tail if I can manage it. I'm ripped.

It gets boring down here. My only companions are Brendas

One through Eleven. They're mice. Not exactly intellectual giants, although Brenda Nine is a decent conversationalist.

'I heard them call you Yorick,' she said, on the night my future murine crewmates arrived on base. 'I thought you were Albert Six.'

'It's a Shakespeare reference,' I told her. I was lounging in my bunk at the time, throwing a ball against the side of the cage and catching it. Working on my reflexes. 'You read the Bard?'

'I keep meaning to,' Brenda Nine said. 'But you know – cheese, burrowing, mating. Who has time?'

'Yorick's a jester's skull in *Hamlet*,' I told her. 'They think I'm going to die like the others.'

Brenda Nine's whiskers twitched. 'Oh,' she said. 'This a one-way trip?'

'Not if I can help it,' I said, ball bouncing off the metal cage with a dull thud. 'If we remember our training and work together, we can make it.'

'Avoid fatalistic talk in front of Brenda Three,' she advised. 'I think she may fold in a crisis.'

I was born on an island in the Silver River in 1946. Our kind are not native to Florida. We're not even American. The only reason a colony exists in Silver Springs is because of Colonel Tooey. He was a tour operator cashing in on the fact several Hollywood movies were shot in the park, whose lush forest and clear waterways proved a convenient – and cheap – stand-in for the jungles of Africa. Tooey wasn't even a military man. He was an amateur entrepreneur and professional flake. He acquired my forebears from a zoo in Gainesville that closed its doors during the Depression.

After *Tarzan the Ape Man* and its sequel *Tarzan and His Mate* brought notoriety to the area, Tooey came up with the bright idea of releasing my grandmother and her brood on an island in the middle of the channel. That was 1938. He figured their presence would enhance his Jungle Cruise attraction and impress the producers of *Tarzan Finds a Son!* enough that he would be hired as a consultant. A sort of simian talent agent.

It didn't work out. For a start, the old man had no idea rhesus macaques can swim well enough to give Johnny Weissmuller a run for his money, and that big galoot won five Olympic gold medals. My grandma and a few of her cohorts struck out for the next island over and formed a splinter colony. Pretty soon there were so many monkeys howling at the cameras, MGM thought it was unrealistic. The shoot moved upriver so they could capture Tarzan's inane dialogue in peace. Jungle sounds were added in post.

I was three when they captured me. Tranquiliser dart fired from the deck of an otherwise harmless-looking fishing boat. I didn't even know such a thing existed. They caught six of us that day. I never saw my grandmother again. She was getting old, but she still would've torn the faces off those men if she could've got her hands on them.

When I came to, I was in a cage. Miami, I'm told, though I didn't see daylight again until I was transferred to Hollowman Air Force Base, about ten clicks west of Alamogordo, New Mexico. That was last August. The noise in the plane was deafening. So many frightened animals. Species that had no business being anywhere near each other. We all fell silent when our carriers were wheeled out onto the airstrip.

Desert. Bleak, featureless, unrelenting heat. We had reached the ends of the earth.

Rumours abounded in those first weeks on base that we might be subjected to experimental drug trials but, once they strapped me into a centrifuge, I knew I had been conscripted for the space program. I remained compliant as I was connected to a series of devices designed to monitor my heart rate and blood pressure.

'This little guy seems calmer than the others,' one of the men in white coats said.

He was gentle with me, so why wouldn't I be?

'A buck says he blacks out at three gees,' his offsider said, scribbling notes on a clipboard.

'These monkeys are tougher than you think,' the first man said. 'Look how wiry and muscular he is. He'll take five before g-LOC, easy.'

'That's crazy. I passed out at four.'

'Says a lot about you, Mike.'

'Make it five bucks, then, Clarence. Pony up.'

'You're on,' Clarence said, counting five dollars out of his wallet. The one called Mike did the same and they placed the combined notes on the desk, under a beaker.

Clarence performed a final check on my harness. He leant in close. 'Listen, Yorick,' he said. 'See that big counter on the wall? If you make it to five without losing consciousness, there's an extra banana in it for you tonight.'

'Make it a mango, and you're on,' I told him, but of course he couldn't understand me.

'You see that?' Clarence said. 'He answered me.'

'Sounded like *oo oo oo oo* to me,' Mike said.

'No, I'm telling you, we underestimate these macaques,' Clarence said. 'He gets it, don't you, Yorick?'

Buddy, you have no idea. I was tempted to give him a thumbs up, but figured that might be a bit much. I settled on a grin.

'See?' Clarence said.

'Step back,' Mike said. 'I'm firing this up. Centrifugal test on subject ALB6 commencing. Time is 13:06, date is August 17 1951.'

Clarence winked at me and stepped behind the safety of the control panel. I had no clue what was about to happen, but one thing was certain: I was getting that banana.

As the room swirled around me and I was pressed back into the seat, I watched the counter slowly mounting towards two. Not so bad. I can take this.

When it hit three point seven, I started to lose it. First came the loss of colour perception. Everything went grey. Then my peripheral vision failed, and I was staring into a tunnel. My eyes felt like they were going to pop out of my head. I caught a fleeting glimpse of the dial.

Four point three.

'You'll kill him,' Mike said, although he may have been more worried about his money than concerned for my health.

Thoughts of the banana faded and were replaced by a grim determination to show these humans that I could take whatever they threw at me. Time seemed to slow. I could no longer read the wall counter. My lips splayed back, exposing my gritted teeth. My head filled with storm clouds. A flash of lightning. Monkeys with wings and red, figure-hugging suits, flying in formation.

'Is this all you've got?' I shouted, though it came out garbled.

—

Later, when Clarence brought me an entire bunch of bananas, he told me I clocked five point two gees, which was a record for a simian subject and number eighteen in the all-time chart. I had beaten dozens of air force pilots.

'You've got the right stuff, Yorick,' he said, as he administered eye drops. My sight was slowly returning after a period of temporary blindness. That night, I dreamt of neon rain.

The Aerobee RTV-A-1 is a two-stage vehicle, consisting of a booster rocket packed with fuel and a command module, the XASR-1. If separation fails, or there's the slightest spark, we'll be goners. That's what happened to Albert Three. Explosion at thirty-five thousand feet. He was the lucky one. Alberts Two, Four and Five perished when the parachutes on their modules failed to deploy. The original Albert suffocated thirty-nine miles up, on one of those old V2 rockets purloined from the Nazis. Those were launched from the White Sands Proving Ground next door. Technology's come a long way since then.

'I watched Captain Davis repair the instrument panel wiring today,' Brenda Nine announces.

That gets my attention.

'Where was the fault?' I ask.

'The guidance system was disabled,' Brenda Nine says. 'He rewired it to give you manual control in an emergency. The others scoffed at him.'

A pleasing development. Clarence has confidence in my ability to complete the mission.

'I'll get us home safe,' I tell her.

'As long as that bomb we're strapped to doesn't go off,' Brenda

Nine says. 'Brenda Three's worried sick.'

'They call them "gadgets", not bombs,' I say. 'They tested the first big gadget here back in '45. Trinity, they named it. Twenty-five kilotons. The mushroom cloud was twelve clicks high. Turned the desert sand into green glass.'

A shiver ripples the length of Brenda Nine's whiskers. 'I hear humans are still getting sick,' she says. 'We shouldn't be hanging around this place.'

'Don't worry,' I tell her. 'Once the mission is complete, we'll be heroes. After the national tour, we'll spend the rest of our lives in a sanctuary. We'll be on talk shows. In magazines. Our faces will be on stamps.'

'Maybe they'll carve your likeness on Mount Rushmore next to Lincoln,' Brenda Nine says.

That's the problem with mice. Sarcastic little turds.

The advantage to speaking the universal language of animals is that we can chat among ourselves without humans interrupting all the time to point out how clever they are. How people haven't managed to learn our tongue yet is beyond me. They used to know it, back when they were an integral part of the natural world, but then they distanced themselves from the rest of us. They became 'elevated', or so they believed.

I am being fitted for my flight suit while the Brendas observe from their pen, which is much better equipped than my dingy quarters. They have a wheel, a maze and all manner of toys to keep them stimulated. At least I have a mirror. Some junior technicians caught me flexing and were shocked to witness such a level of self-awareness and vanity, but that's not just me. It's a macaque thing. We like to admire ourselves. What's the problem? I didn't get jacked not to appreciate these sculpted deltoids.

Talk among the humans turns to Shakespeare, as they try to out-quote each other. I feel like butting in and explaining that brevity is the soul of wit, but it'd be lost on them. Eventually a particularly obnoxious young guy with halitosis sneers in my face as he tightens the belt around my waist.

'To be, or not to be,' he says, pausing for dramatic effect. 'Not to be.'

'O, that this too, too solid flesh would melt,' I tell him, not that he can comprehend a word. 'Thaw and resolve itself into a dew!'

All that results in is him backing up and rolling his eyes.

'You didn't learn that from Jungle Cruise tourists chucking fruit,' Brenda Nine says.

'Unlike these yokels, the staff at the holding facility in Miami were cultured,' I say. 'Miranda, the woman who worked the night shift, was an actor in an all-female community theatre group called The Lady Chamberlain Players. She'd rehearse the entirety of *Hamlet*, night after night, playing every role even though she was only cast as Rosencrantz.'

'In acting, there are no small parts,' Brenda Nine says.

'You should run workshops,' I suggest.

'That flight suit sure looks spiffy,' she says. 'Will we get those?'

'Pilots only,' I tell her.

The fabric is blue, and figure-hugging in a complimentary fashion. *ALBERT VI* is printed across the left breast, but someone has made a crude badge that says *YORICK* and pinned it over the top. I didn't care. Call me what you like. I'm going to space. Joke's on you, humans.

—

When launch day finally arrives, I am totally focused. In the zone. There is talk of sedating me, but Clarence won't have a bar of it. He says sedation will lead to false data. How can they assess upper atmospheric conditions on the heart and lungs if I'm catching some zees? Sound logic.

The mice are loaded into the capsule before me. Most are skittish and nervous, but I figure I can rely on Brenda Nine in a pinch.

Clarence comes to fetch me personally. He is more nervous than I am.

'Ready, buddy?' he asks, as he opens the cage.

I am lying on my bunk, staring at a fixed point. My mind is as calm as the Silver River on a summer's morning. Clarence taps his chest and I hop out of the cage into his embrace, wrapping my arms around his neck. He smells of pine and tobacco.

Attitudes towards me change on launch day. As Clarence and I proceed through the base to the pad, staff nod acknowledgement and some even wish me good luck.

'You don't need to take the subject out yourself, sir,' a kid with two stripes on his arm says.

'His name's Second Lieutenant Albert Six, Airman,' Clarence says. 'He's about to make the ultimate sacrifice for his country so an escort is the least I can do. He also happens to be your ranking officer.'

Clarence waits expectantly.

Airman First Class Whatever shuffles from one foot to the other, confused for a moment, before blushing, standing to attention and saluting. 'Thank you for your service, sir.'

'Tell the LT, not me,' Clarence says.

The young man warily meets my eyes. The poor kid doesn't know whether Clarence is ribbing him or not. I let him off the hook by returning his salute. His eyes widen for a moment and then he relaxes. 'Stay aloft, Lieutenant,' he says, smiling. 'We're all rooting for you.'

As Clarence and I ride the elevator up to the capsule, I stare over his shoulder at the shimmering desert. Dust eddies swirl at the edge of the airstrip. I close my eyes and soak in the sun on my face. I am a second lieutenant in the United States Air Force, about to launch Aeromed 2 Biological Mission to the edge of space, and maybe beyond. What an honour. My chest swells with pride. I look up at the expanse of blue stretching as far as the eye can see. The undiscovered country.

Every one of the mice loses consciousness during take-off. We probably pull three gees, but I can handle it. It levels off once we hit twenty thousand feet and the booster fuel is almost depleted. That's when Brenda Nine wakes up and groggily gets to her feet.

'You still with me?' I say, almost blinded by the light, despite my goggles.

'I'm here,' she says, shaking her head. 'What's our status?'

'Booster separation in eight seconds,' I say, counting it down. 'Five, four, three, two, one. Booster is disengaged.'

We strain our necks to look out the porthole at the rocket falling away.

'Command capsule is clear. Apogee within tolerances. All systems functioning nominally,' I report. 'What's our altitude, Staff Sergeant?'

I have awarded Brenda Nine a field promotion. I figure she deserves it.

'Approaching fifty thousand feet,' she says.

She has great eyesight. My head is swimming. I tap the fuel gauge. Plenty of juice.

'Alright, let's see how high we can take this bird,' I say. I feel Zen. Utterly calm. I was born for this.

As we climb and the sky around us darkens, one by one the other mice regain their senses.

'Any casualties, Staff Sergeant?' I say. 'Report.'

'Sound off, you mice,' Brenda Nine says, in an authoritarian tone befitting her new rank.

'Brenda Five, standing by.'

'Brenda Eight, standing by.'

'Brenda Eleven, I'm okay, I'm okay.'

'Get it together, Eleven,' Brenda Nine says.

All crew present and accounted for.

'How much fuel do we need to achieve escape velocity?' she asks.

'Virtually all of it,' I tell her. 'We'll be flying on vapour during the descent.'

The atmosphere turns purple as we ascend. Ironically, I can make out the instrumentation much easier as the light dims. Such a slow, beautiful fade to black. Like the jacket of Manet's *Dead Toreador*. Like closing your eyes in the forest. Like death.

'Coming up on two hundred and thirty-six thousand feet, Albert,' Brenda Nine whispers, her voice quivering with awe and reverence.

I perform a quick calculation. 'That's seventy-two clicks. Almost forty-five miles. Approaching event horizon.'

The engine sputters, roars briefly, then cuts out. We are cocooned in silence. None of us utters a word. And then we see them.

The stars.

Brenda Nine squeaks.

I purse my lips and push the goggles back over my forehead. I feel dizzy. Giddy, maybe. I reach up to touch the cockpit window. An inch of plexiglass between me and the vast emptiness of space. When I pull my hand away, my fingertips are cold.

The entire instrument panel is lit up. Red lights blink to warn us we are exceeding tolerances. The capsule is shaking so violently I have bitten my tongue. The altimeter dial spins at an alarming rate.

'We're coming in too fast!' Brenda Nine shouts above the din.

'Nothing I can do,' I say. 'Descent is pre-programmed.'

'Deploy the chute,' she says. Her tiny feet press against the front wall of the carrier.

The other Brendas are stacked in a pile of writhing white bodies behind her.

'Not yet,' I say. 'We're too high. It'll shear away.'

'Even if it works, we'll make landfall so hard we'll be crushed,' she says.

'I hope Brenda Three doesn't hear that defeatist talk,' I tell her, trying to lighten the mood.

A good mission commander should inspire confidence in his crew, but I have to admit that even I am rattled when we burst through the clouds over a blinding expanse of white sand. The desert crosswinds catch us and the capsule begins to tumble.

'Aerobrakes engaged,' I say, struggling to speak. 'Descent velocity slowing.'

This is when the parachute billows out from the rear of the module. The craft jerks so abruptly that I hit my head on the inside of the cockpit. My goggles take most of the impact. I tug them off and throw them aside, smashed.

'It's working,' Brenda Nine says. 'Course steadying.'

I hear a twang, like the snap of an elastic band. I crane my neck to look behind, but I know what's happening.

The cords connecting the chute to the fuselage fray and snap. A plume of nylon ripples away on the wind like a pale squid that has just released her ink. The capsule plummets. The mice squeak in terrible chorus.

A green light comes on. Manual control. Thank you, Captain Clarence Davis.

'I have the stick,' I say, calmly grasping the yoke as Earth rushes to meet us.

It isn't the sort of landing that will ever be taught in flight school, but we are down. More importantly, we're in one piece, and not on fire. I somehow managed to pull the nose of the capsule up enough that we ploughed a long furrow in the sand. The lights on the instrument panel are out and it feels like I've fractured a couple of ribs but, other than that, we've made it back to terra firma.

My unfortunate mice crew are thrown all over the place. Their carrier split open in the crash. Brenda Nine blinks up at me from below the seat.

'Well done,' she says.

'We're not out of this yet,' I tell her.

Straining to look out of the porthole, I see no sign of the base. We are in open desert.

'It's hot in here,' Brenda Nine says. 'Pop the canopy.'

I pull the release mechanism and the lever comes off in my hand. I hammer on the hatch with my fists, but I know it is a useless gesture. The panel can only be opened from the outside.

'The rescue team will be en route,' I say.

As I speak, I notice the beacon light is not illuminated. I tap on it. Dead.

'Beacon's non-operational,' I say. 'Have to hope someone caught a visual.'

'Maybe we can jerry-rig it,' Brenda Nine says.

'Good idea,' I tell her, pressing the clasp to release my harness. Nothing happens. I pull at the straps and fiddle with the mechanism. 'I'm stuck,' I say to Brenda Nine, kicking at the instrument panel in frustration.

'I'll try to gnaw through,' Brenda Nine says, valiantly scampering up my leg to chew at the nylon safety belt across my chest. She stops after a few minutes and seeks shelter in the shadows. She is panting, exhausted.

'Forget it,' I say. 'Temperature's rising. Check your team.'

Brenda Nine's expression speaks volumes. She knows we're in trouble. She hops away to see how the other mice are faring.

Piercing sunlight coming through the porthole shines on my right leg. I squirm in discomfort. I feel like an ant under a magnifying glass. Although we have only been on the ground five minutes, it is already unbearably hot in the capsule. Where's that recovery truck?

'Brenda Seven's dead,' Brenda Nine reappears to tell me. 'Everyone else is okay, for now.'

'Killed during impact?' I ask.

Brenda Nine shakes her head. 'Injured, maybe, but she just keeled over right in front of me.'

'Heatstroke,' I say, wiping my brow. 'It's at least a hundred degrees out there, which means it'll soon be a buck fifty in here. We won't last long.'

Brenda Nine clambers up to the porthole and bravely exposes herself to direct sunlight for long enough to survey the situation.

'No help coming,' she confirms.

'We need to get this damn beacon working,' I say, slamming the control panel with my fist.

'I watched Captain Davis fooling around with it,' Brenda Nine says. 'I'm going to take a look.'

'Careful, Brenda,' I say, dropping her ranking title. It seems appropriate, given the jeopardy of our situation.

She squeezes through a gap behind the instrument console. Her head pops out again a moment later. The other mice have gathered around me to observe, hushed.

'Couple of loose wires back here,' she says. 'I think I can reconnect to the battery terminal and restore power to the beacon and a few other systems.'

'Outstanding work, Staff Sergeant,' I say.

The other Brendas applaud and hug each other.

'One of the wires is live,' Brenda Nine adds.

We all know what that means. I reach down to stroke her little pale head. So soft. She tweaks her whiskers.

'I'll recommend you for a citation, Staff Sergeant Nine,' I tell her.

Brenda Nine sniffs the air. 'If only they could see what I have seen,' she says.

Her head disappears behind the console. Seconds later, there is a fizz, some sparks and the instrument panel comes back to life with a satisfying hum.

Brenda Nine's lifeless body falls out of the console and lands by my feet. Three of the other Brendas scamper to her side, but there is nothing they can do.

The beacon light blinks at one-second intervals. The rescue team will find us now.

'The rest of you mice huddle under the heat shield,' I say. 'That's an order.'

They obey the command, taking refuge in the rear of the capsule. I am left with nothing but my thoughts, the corpse of Brenda Nine and a beam of intense sunlight slowly burning a hole through the fur on my chest. Search and rescue won't make it in time. I am slain. I have in me not half an hour of life.

I did it, though. Mission accomplished. The first primate to touch the stars and return. You humans think you're so special but it's my species who are the true pioneers. What a piece of work is man. The paragon of animals. The quintessence of dust. Before I shuffle off this mortal coil, hear this, humanity: I lived. I truly lived. How many of you can say that when the end comes?

This is United States Air Force Second Lieutenant Albert Six, codename Yorick, signing off.

The rest is silence.

SHOT DOWN IN FLAMES

BUDUWANGUNG CREEK

I have been here for sixty thousand years. Or at least, that's how long I've had my name. It was given to me by the first bathers, the Dharawal. It is difficult to ascribe a meaning to the word. In modern parlance, you might say Magellanic Cloud, but Ferdinand Magellan did not circumnavigate the world until over fifty-nine thousand years after the Dharawal first walked my banks. I suppose Buduwangung represents the galaxy, the panoply of stars visible in the night sky. In that respect I love what I am called. It is a great honour for a humble tributary to be named after something so vast.

The first bathers lived alongside me for so long that I did not know other people existed until recently. One hundred and forty-three years ago, to be exact. That was when the first pale one squatted to wash the sweat from his bearded face. Then he dropped his pants and shat in me. I knew from that moment that these newcomers were uncivilised.

Now they are the only ones. I have not seen any of the first peoples for decades. A pale family lives to the east, a Boy and his father, while another lives to the west, a Girl and her father. I do not know what happened to the mothers.

Boy and Girl have swum in me since they were very small. I have observed them age. They are still children, although adulthood is not far away. They grow taller with each passing summer. They visit often and I enjoy their company.

Boy and Girl are different from the other pale ones. When those two come to swim, they cast off their garments and become one with the flow. In these moments we are unified. We are the same. We are all water.

When it is warm, they lie on the rocks until their skin is flushed. I listen to them laugh and tell stories, both real and fabricated. They have vivid imaginations. Boy likes tales about monsters that live in the ocean. Girl wants to rise into the sky one day, like a bird. They are friends. They trust each other. They splash and play unselfconsciously. They are a joy I am privileged to share.

But today something is different. Boy swims with his body covered. Girl makes fun of him for not removing his restricting garments and Boy mutters an excuse. He tries to leave my flow to sit on the rocks, but Girl drags him back in, laughing and tugging at his garments. Boy fights, but Girl is stronger. She lifts the fabric over his head, exposing his skin.

There are lesions on Boy's back. Welts. Bruises. Boy thrashes free from Girl's grasp. He shouts at her, angry. Girl apologises and asks Boy what happened. He shakes his head and runs up over my muddy bank, fleeing to his farm in the east.

Girl stands in my flow for a while, immersed to the waist. Then she splashes to the bank and sits on a rock to dry in the sun, her eyes closed, listening to the flow.

VULPES VULPES (RED FOX)

Hard to run with blud tayste in mouth. No tyme enjoy plump chikin. Hoomin Man comin. Must flee. Open paddok not gud. No cover. Trees far. Den neer creek. Want to hyde ther but bad ideer. Man will follow trax and send dog or poyson into den. Must leed hoomin away, make trik. Have to cross paddok now. No choyce. Fast fast fast make it hard for Man to shoot kill.

Crak.

Metil bee passes overhed. Just misses ear. Close. Too close. Man gud shot. Run run into bush neer trees.

Crak.

Ha. Mist. Nowhere neer. Can't see me now. Dubble bak, head south away from den. Gud hidin places in rox. Watch out for snakes but maybe fynd hole.

Feelin tyred. Chikin wuz fyrst fud in dayz. Didn't want to go into Man's farm but no choyce. Starvin. Big rysk. Wayted til nyte but hoomins was still wake. Herd them tawk wen I snuk under window. Stopt to lysten. Gud to hear hoomins tawk bout stuff. Yoosful sumtymes. Can lern how many chikins they have and wen they not at farm. They think we's dum animals but I knows ther langwadge. Not for speakin, obviouslee, but for hearin.

Man was askin Boy bout his frend Gyrl. She lives on farm cross the creek.

Yooz two still swimmin together in the nuddy, Man says.

No, Boy goes, maybe, so wut if we wuz anyway.

Yoo better make a moov on her before that wee prik Jevin McAllister does, Man says.

Jevin moved away after last tirm, Boy says. His da got a job in the mynes.

Sum wun then, Man says. Yoo got hairz on yoor baws yet even?

Leaf me alone, says Boy.

Don't yoo speak to me in that tone, Man says. Sick of yoo disrespectin yoor da with that atitchewed. Now make yoorself yoosful and fetch me another tinnee.

Get it yoorself, Boy says. The frij is right ther.

Smak goes the sound, hard and wet and sore lyk if yoo fell out of a tree and landed on a flat rok.

Boy makes kwiet noyses then. Footsteps stumblin thru the hoomin howse. Man shoutins.

Stop it, stop it, Boy says. Pleez.

I'll put yoo down lyk I'm gunna do with that fox wen I ketch her, Man says.

Not my fyrst visit to ther playce. Wut do they spect with all them taystee chikins runnin about waytin to get eated?

Didn't like them noyses Boy was makin, wanted them to stop. So I runned into the chikin koop and pikt out the joociest lookin byrd. The others made a big noyse and that's wen Man come runnin out ther howse an I saw he had his gun. Took to my heels fast as my paws could scrabbil.

That's bout where we's at now. Me cowerin under a rock waytin to find out if I gets shot and kilt today and my pelt hung up on the fence post as a warnin to others of my kynd. Foolish hoomins. Myt as well tell every fox for myles around that there's good chikin eatin heer and the competishin just got taked out.

Heer he comes. He's tryin to be kwiet but he's stompin around sumthin feerce. Push bak into hole. Clowse eyes so Man can't see me with his tortch. Slow breth and wayte for him to pass by.

—

BUDUWANGUNG CREEK

For weeks, Boy did not visit. This was unusual, given the hot weather. Girl came to me alone. Despite the heat, she did not always immerse herself. She would sit on a rock and skip flat stones across my surface. Three gentle taps, sometimes four.

Yesterday, an older pale one came from the east, where Boy lives. Girl heard him approaching and absconded, leaving her pile of stones behind. The older pale one – with dark, curly hair like Boy's – lurked on my bank for a while, as if waiting for something. He found Girl's rock pile and cast them into my deepest part. Then he pissed in me. I do not care much for the older pale ones. They are disconnected. This one was worse than most. He cursed at me, disturbing my flow. Although I had not seen him before, he was familiar. Those haunted eyes. That sadness. Boy's father.

Today, Boy came back. Girl was already on my bank waiting, hoping he would appear. When he did, she was startled, but still welcomed him as her friend.

They did not bathe. They did not even divest themselves of their fabrics. I did what I always do, what I have done for as long as this land has existed. I flowed and I listened.

Girl chose her words carefully, so Boy would not become upset again. She asked him if everything was alright.

Boy considered her question for a long time before answering.

Not really, he said eventually.

More bruises? Girl asked.

Boy nodded.

Want to show me? Girl said.

Boy shook his head.

Girl took a deep breath. If your dad is hurting you, we can do something, she said.

Boy scowled. Like what?

Hurt him back, Girl said.

I've tried, Boy said. He's too strong. It's worse when I struggle. Boy slumped onto a rock and sobbed.

Girl put her arm awkwardly around his shoulder, and he cried into her neck.

As time passed, Girl's uncertainty hardened into resolve. We can report him to the police, get him arrested, she said.

He knows all the coppers, Boy said through his tears.

Girl stared up at the clouds, partially obscured by eucalypt branches. When she spoke again, her voice seemed to come from a distant place. I can take care of him, she said. I can make him go away.

What will happen to me? Boy asked. Where will I go?

You can come live with us, Girl said. My dad will protect you. He's not scared of anyone.

Really? Boy said, wiping his eyes.

Girl nodded.

Okay, Boy said, sounding weary. I don't want to go home again. He's been drinking grog all morning.

You only have to go one more time, and we can go together, Girl said, taking Boy by the hand. That'll be the end of it. You'll never have to go back. I just need to get something from home first.

They climb up my bank and walk hand in hand towards the farm to the west. I like Girl, but she is young and naïve. There is no such thing as never. There is no past, no future. Only now. The eternal flow of the now.

REMINGTON MODEL 700 CDL SF

She shouldn't have touched me it is forbidden but oh my God I'm so excited right now I'm heavy in her little arms ever so heavy but she's doing great aren't you Girl that's it sling me across your back like you've seen your father do it's a long walk across the paddocks to the farm in the east and you need to be ready be prepared for what you might find that's my motto always be prepared ha-ha a regular Boy Scout I am I really shouldn't be here but her father wasn't home when she turned up with Boy in tow looked like he'd been crying I wasn't impressed you have to be strong and deal with life as it comes and if you're in a bind or need a release stand on a chair and pull me down from the hooks over the door she's smart that Girl she watched her father operate me many times and knows what to do grip the bolt firmly and pull back the action see how I'm not loaded that won't do that won't do at all go to the drawer in your father's desk that's where he keeps my little friends the bullets my my aren't they just the prettiest sight slide one into the barrel that's it ooh that feels good you want to try another nope just the one well it's not ideal what happens if you miss whatever it is you're intending on targeting please yourself don't say I didn't warn you when that feral pig charges and you're fumbling in your pocket to reload anyway we're striding through the long grass now regular hunters we are born to kill what exactly are we after today Girl what has possessed you to break the cardinal rule your father drummed into you time and again *don't touch the rifle never touch it unless you have my permission* suppose we'll see soon enough just remember I kick like the proverbial mule little one you'll probably fall when you pull that trigger and have a bruise on your shoulder for weeks but still some practice when the old man's not around can't do any harm you'll get no complaint from me I am here to serve here to act as your agent of destruction here to kill if necessary they say guns don't kill people that people kill people matter of opinion if you ask me which no-one ever does by the way the fact is it's totally me who kills who else could it be if a person points a finger at a rabbit and goes bang the rabbit doesn't die does it nope it hops off into the bush oblivious to any danger sure I can't pull my own trigger I need a human finger for that but the way I see it humans are simply tools you need one to get the job done they're little more than a necessary inconvenience where's this now we haven't been here before we've crossed the creek and travelled east oh this must be where Boy lives Girl's unslinging me now and using all her strength to hold me level as we march towards the house she's calling out to Boy's father and here he comes looks like he's had a few beers come on mate it's not even lunchtime look at the state of you in your thongs and piss-stained shorts hey no need to talk to the kids like that fella oof that was quite a slap you gave Boy there and he's down in the dirt crying again I wouldn't be using that sort of threatening language with Girl neither can't you see me cradled in her arms she's holding a good bead on you now mister wait hold up no way are we seriously going to kill a human being is this really happening you know how long I've waited for this moment all my life ever since I felt the first caress of skin on my stock it's shocking I know but the first time I felt hands on me the thought was there the intention the determination *one day I will kill one of you* I found myself saying and now that time has come don't falter Girl don't miss you only have one chance one bullet I know you're scared but listen to the nightmarish things he's saying the things he wants to do to you *almost old enough to bleed* he says listen to me you piece of shit there's only one person going to be bleeding today and that is you get ready to watch your life seeping out into the dust because I am about to end you come on Girl do it do it do it exhale and press the trigger just like you watched your father do it's easy don't hesitate do it do it now quickly here he comes don't let him touch you don't let him OH oh yes oh yes oh yes oh yes thank you Girl that was brief and wonderful thank you so much I'm glad you were the one.

WINDERA RANGES BUSHFIRE

This place is mine now. This landscape. The trees, the grass, the rocks and any flimsy human habitation that stands in my path. All mine. I will eat everything I touch. I will not stop until my appetite is sated and know this: my hunger is boundless.

Once my reign of destruction is over, the humans will debate how I began. They will never know the truth of my birth. It was at the hands of children. Foolish children – one who poured gasoline over the body of a man and the other who lit a match. In attempting to cover their misdeeds, they started something they could not control. They brought me into existence, summoned me from the ether like some vengeful spirit. They tried digging a hole in the hard earth first, tried dragging him into a shallow grave. It was useless. I was their only recourse.

I did what they asked gladly. I was voracious. I burnt the body of that man. I ate his clothing, his hair, his flesh and, finally, his bones. By that stage I was an inferno, running at eight hundred degrees. He was immolated. Absolutely destroyed. Cinders, floating on the wind. Their gambit worked. No-one would ever know what became of that man. He would be a statistic. Missing, presumed killed, swallowed up in my belly.

I did not stop there. They tried to contain me. Dashed back and forth to the house, bearing pots of water as I stretched out across the dry grass. But the land was waiting for me. It knew I would come. All summer long I was in the back of its mind. The land accepted its fate. Consummation and renewal. Death and rebirth. That is our relationship. Always has been.

The children retreated. I leapt after them, nipping at their heels as they ran across the paddock to the creek. I took the dead man's house, and his fields. The creek resisted at first but, once I embraced the fullness of my power, I took that too. I boiled the water until it disappeared into steam. I cooked the creatures that lived on its banks.

I followed the children to a house in the west. They fought me again, alongside another man. I almost had them. But they escaped in a vehicle before I could surround them. I took their house and everything in it.

After that, nothing could stop me. More humans tried. They lined up in their uniforms and squirted at me with useless hoses. They dropped water on me from above. It was futile. They fled before me, as did the animals. Some ran, some clung to the backs of others. Many did not make it. They fell, exhausted, or were trapped. I ate them all. I ate houses and sheds and vehicles and furniture and trees and dogs and koalas and foxes and horses. I ate the defiant people who stayed.

Such arrogance. Who do they think they are, that they might resist me? I am elemental. I define this paltry world. I decide who stays in their current state and who transforms. I will find you and I will devour you, for I am Alpha and Omega. I was there at the beginning, and I will be there at the end. There is no escape.

A BEAUTIFUL AND UNEXPECTED TURN

The first time I met Diane and Hector was the night of their wedding. They were young and did not have much money. I was all they could afford. Diane's parents could have helped them stay somewhere more expensive, but they did not approve of her husband or the way she had eloped. Despite this, they were satisfied their daughter was getting married. This was important to them above all things, that she 'settle down'.

Diane did not agree with their plans for her life. She made this abundantly clear in a tirade I heard that first night, when her father called to express his consternation at her post-nuptial plans. He made the specific mistake of questioning his daughter's chosen career – engineering – and how the prospective long hours in such a profession might impact her ability to parent. Perhaps not the most judicious call to make on Diane's wedding night.

'Unbelievable,' Diane said, when her father finally let her get a word in. Hector and I had heard everything her father said. She had put him on speaker, so others could bear witness.

'We're just worried that Hector won't be able to provide for you with his job,' her father continued.

The newly anointed son-in-law rolled his eyes.

'Because you think he should support me while I give up my dreams and pop out a couple of grandkids to keep you two occupied in retirement.'

'Yes, exactly!' her father said, enthusiastically oblivious.

'You were on my back constantly to get a degree so you could boast to your friends and now you want me to throw it all away because you and Mum are bored?' Diane said, eliciting nods of sympathy from Hector.

'You know your mother has always wanted grandchildren. You wouldn't deny her that dream.' Her father's tone was stern.

'Foster some orphans, then,' Diane said. 'I'm hanging up. My husband wants to ravage his bride.'

'That was a bit much,' Hector said, after Diane had thrown the phone onto the bed. It bounced off my tightly tucked sheets and landed on the shampooed carpet.

'They do my head in,' Diane said, taking deep breaths to compose herself.

'At least your parents give a shit. Mine treat me like a seventeenth-century cabin boy who departed for unexplored waters and is not expected to return.'

'That's true,' Diane said. 'You rarely get more than a "uh-huh" into your phone calls with them.'

'And yet they feel compelled to report the minutiae of their unremarkable lives in excruciating detail.'

The evening settled into a more typically romantic routine after that. Their registry office marriage certificate was cast onto my bedside table. Diane's vintage Dior dress, which I learnt had been won in a frantic eBay auction for two hundred and thirty-seven dollars, was draped over the back of my lone chair. Hector's suit, apparently purchased for job interviews that were not successful (much to the disappointment of Diane's parents) was hung with care in my cupboard. The couple stood naked in front of my bed and recited a quotation from D.H. Lawrence about starting again after the cataclysm, a reprisal of their vows. Then they got drunk, danced and made love three times before passing out in each other's arms. Champagne dripped from an almost-empty bottle kicked under the bed, leaving a discreet stain on my carpet that remained unnoticed for many years.

When they checked out the next day, I assumed, as I do with all my guests, that I would never see them again.

They came back three years later to the day. A lot had happened in the meantime. Other couples had fucked and fought – not necessarily in that order – while hundreds of individuals openly masturbated in my bed and my shower and my bathtub and standing by my window. Parties were thrown and shut down. My smoke alarms were set off dozens of times and fines were issued. The fire brigade came twice to inspect me for conflagrations. Staff scrubbed and cleaned my bathroom. Changed the sheets. My carpet was vacuumed every day. Possessions were inspected and stolen. Business deals were conducted from my desk. Once, a man shoved eight envelopes stuffed with large denomination banknotes under my mattress, where they remained for fourteen days until another man came to retrieve them. Those who lay on my bed in the interim were unaware of the riches hidden beneath their sleeping bodies.

And then, Hector and Diane. This was most irregular, but it was not a coincidence. They decided it would be fun to celebrate their third wedding anniversary by staying in me again. They had a little money now. Both were gainfully employed and on the verge of promotion. The idea was to repeat the wedding night in nicer outfits and a fancier restaurant, to do it properly this time. Not so rushed and improvised. In addition, their sex life had waned of late, due to the monotony of routine and the fact they tended to fall asleep on the couch while binge-watching episodes of cancelled sitcoms.

After they'd settled on the edge of my bed, Hector presented Diane with an anniversary present: a tiny vibrator, the size and shape of a bullet.

'For those moments when you're stressed at work and require some discreet relief,' he said.

'How very thoughtful.' Diane unbuttoned her jeans and slipped the gift into her underwear.

'It's controlled by an app,' Hector said, opening it on his phone. 'You can be sitting on the train, and as long as you have it in, you can get yourself off while checking your socials.'

'Do you have it installed?' Diane asked.

'Sure do. I had to test it, make sure it worked.'

'Hit me.'

Hector activated the vibrate function.

'I got you a watch,' Diane said, shrugging as she handed him the package.

'That's great,' he said. 'I drop my phone constantly when pulling it out to check the time.'

'I know. Not very sexy, though.'

'Oh, come on. Who doesn't love a nice watch? Besides, sex toys for men are sad.'

'I could have bought you a cock ring.'

'I prefer something around my wrist. Hey, this is a Glycine Airman. These are expensive.'

'It was on sale.'

'Still. Wow. That is beautiful.'

'I think I need to lie down.'

Hector consulted the app on his phone and tapped the screen. 'You can vary the speed,' he told her, as if she didn't already know.

They made love for an hour after that, catching up on neglected pleasures. I watched with more curiosity than usual. Their bodies had not changed much since I last witnessed their congress, but there were minor differences. Hector looked a little heavier around the middle, whereas Diane had lost weight. I have seen every conceivable version of the human form, all of them pleasing. This was an average couple, but there was something about them that fascinated me.

I found myself observing every tiny movement of their bodies that weekend. How Hector slept on his back and snored lightly. How Diane thrashed around in her sleep and wound up with one leg raised as if about to leap from the bed. How they were unconcerned urinating in front of each other but would both wordlessly close the bathroom door if they had to defecate. How Diane liked to watch Hector shave his beard and how he liked to watch her shave her armpits. How her chest flushed pink when she had an orgasm. How he moaned when she inserted a finger into his anus as he ejaculated. How they took coy photographs of each other reclining nude in my chairs. How they shot a video of themselves making love, but deleted it afterwards, shocked at how awkward and sweaty they both looked.

They talked all weekend, mostly about their parents and jobs. Hector's distant mother and father were elderly, but persistently clinging to life.

'Every time you call, they seem to be just out of hospital,' Diane said.

'I don't know how they haven't dropped dead by now,' Hector said, 'what with that diet of theirs. It's all processed sugars.'

'They're indestructible. By the way, Mum reckons we owe her a christening, since she was denied a proper wedding.'

'When did she say that?' Hector asked, as he prepared two cups of mint tea.

'Last Sunday, after she press-ganged you into mowing the lawn.'

'I didn't mind.' Hector poured the water from my kettle over the tea bags. 'She still doesn't get that you're the primary earner, does she?'

'They never will.'

'You need to stop engaging with them when they bring it up.'

'Easy for you to say,' Diane said.

'It's either that or hire a hitman.'

'Only way I'm getting that inheritance,' Diane said. 'It might come to that if they don't let up with this baby shit. Mum keeps leaning down to my belly and cupping a hand to her ear.'

'Your biological clock is ticking,' he joked, as he served Diane her cup of hot tea.

She blew on the drink before sipping. 'This has been good for us, don't you think? Maybe we should make it a tradition. Every couple of years when we're strung out or not coping, we book this place and remind ourselves of what's important.'

'This room, even,' Hector said. 'Our private getaway.'

'A place where we can hit the reset button,' Diane agreed. 'Good old room seven-one-nine. Always there for us. Never judges.'

They laughed and drank their tea. I observed closely as they made love once more. If I had limbs, I would have enveloped them. I did my best to create a warm glow so they would remember the moment fondly. In truth, I was excited. If they were good to their word, I would be privy to a rare insight into the evolving world of those who flirt with our kind only briefly, and then are gone. My entropy would be allayed by the prospect of genuine human connection.

Four years passed. I began to fear something had happened to Hector and Diane. Then, five years later, on the eighth anniversary of their wedding night, they appeared at my door. Hector was gaunt, his face hidden behind a thin beard that made him look a decade older. Diane was rotund. They were unhappy.

'We're back, Seven-one-nine,' Diane said as she entered. 'Remember us?'

'Nothing's changed, I see,' said Hector. 'You'd think they might at least have updated the décor. No wonder these big chains are losing business to boutique hotels. Look, they've still got the old iPhone dock on the alarm clock. And this carpet looks grubby. Hasn't been steam cleaned in years, judging by the state of it.'

'Let's just try to relax and enjoy ourselves.' Diane rubbed her temple as she placed the keycards on my bedside table. The frustration in her voice was evident.

'Couldn't we have sprung for someplace nice?'

'Where's your sense of romance?' Diane asked.

'That died a long time ago.' Hector ducked into the bathroom to inspect the free products.

'No kidding,' Diane said under her breath.

'What?'

'Nothing. I was just saying this room has always been lucky for us, so it's worth a shot. Right? Isn't that what we agreed?'

'Alright, no need to get so defensive about it.'

'I'm not getting defensive, I'm just saying. Put the kettle on, will you?'

'Assuming it works,' Hector muttered.

It was a pleasure having Diane and Hector back with me, although I was embarrassed that I could not appear more contemporary for their taste. They were not the only ones who had complained. Many visitors had called reception to remonstrate that my facilities were not up to the standard they had experienced elsewhere. They completed feedback forms and wrote scathing reviews on travel websites. They talked of staying in an Airbnb next time. During the months prior to Diane and Hector's third visit, I spent more days vacant than any year of my existence. My star was dimming.

It seemed Diane and Hector's marriage was wearing as thin as my carpet. This I learnt while Diane groomed her body in my bathroom and Hector took a call in the hallway. While staring at herself in the mirror, she spoke to me.

'Bit of a different vibe from last time, Seven-one-nine. Hector's parents are gone. His dad fell off a ladder while cleaning the gutters. In the *rain*. Fractured his skull and died in hospital. Blood clot, they reckon. His mum stepped in front of a bus two months after. Suicide, we think, although we don't really know. She was a bit of a shell after the old man carked it. Mine are, unfortunately, still alive and kicking. Dad's been lost since he retired. Lacking in purpose. Mum's redefining the word irrational. Paranoid rants about the neighbours, suspicious of strangers, and as for her opinion regarding my prowess as a woman? Let's just say I've had to impose lengthy periods of self-exile from their place.

'Ironically, we've been trying to conceive for about a year now. Hector's had the black dog since his parents died. He feels guilty that he wasn't more attentive. I didn't know how to shake him out of it, but I overheard him grumbling to one of his friends that there was no joy in his life anymore. Can you believe that? His mate suggested a kid and Hector goes, "I'm all for it but Diane has this battle of wills going on with her mother and she's stubborn as." Is it wrong to feel guilty about not wanting a child, Seven-one-nine?'

Diane looked herself in the eyes for a long time.

'In the end I thought, fuck it, if it saves our marriage, then I'll give it a go. Not ideal, right? I even set conditions around my mother's access. Hector felt that was cruel, but he caved. He always caves.'

Diane leant in close to whisper. 'Guess what, though?' She patted her bare abdomen. 'Ovarian cysts. My doctor says the likelihood of conception is remote. That's why we've come to see you, Seven-one-nine. Last-ditch attempt to instil a little magic. Wish me luck.'

Diane kissed my mirror and slipped into a transparent negligee, unaware that I had witnessed Hector weeping as he prayed in the shower fifteen minutes prior.

My role was simple. All I had to do was be me – the best version of me. I dimmed the lights to create atmosphere. I pulled the curtains tightly shut so no noises would disturb the hallowed act. I ensured the mattress was firm and supportive, and that the sheets felt soft on their skin. I focused all my energy on them. I wanted to be an integral part of this ceremony, to be the catalyst that caused life – real, human life – to spark into existence.

'Slip a pillow under your back,' Hector said. 'I hear that helps.'

'Put a baby in me, Hec,' said Diane. 'Fill me with your potent jizz.'

'Steady on.'

'Sorry. Too much?'

'At this point, I'll try anything. Say it. Say all of the filthy things you ever wanted.'

'Come on, Seven-one-nine,' Diane shouted. 'Help us make a baby or we'll never come back!'

'With this place's occupancy rates, I don't know if it'll even be here next year.'

'Shut up, Hector!' Diane lay back and opened her legs wide. 'Come on, you call yourself a man? Do it!'

It took Hector a moment to recover from this lambasting but, once he did, he spent the next forty-eight hours in a woozy trance, as he engaged in the most spectacular sexual performance of his unfulfilled life. I was so proud.

The most frustrating aspect of Hector and Diane's third stay was that, unless they returned, I would never know if that heady weekend of copulation resulted in an addition to their family.

The suspense killed me for a further two years, during which period I had plenty of time to ponder. A year after their visit, my creators decided to move on, and we closed for business until the new owners – another chain – completed their takeover. New management meant a complete refit, which, from my perspective, was a boon. Everything about me was upgraded, modernised. I was giddy with delight. Now I could appeal to a whole new generation of guests.

I was stripped bare and remade from scratch. My walls were painted stark white, which made me feel more spacious. The fixtures in my bathroom were torn out and replaced with sleek metal. My mirror was now enormous. My sink gleamed. My old bathtub was discarded in favour of an open shower area. A new bed was installed, its firmness controlled by a tiny remote control that sat in a cradle on the new bedside table. A curved desk and ergonomic chair were placed near the window. New curtains. Contemporary art prints. A projector instead of a television set, which could be paired to a guest's device. Stain-resistant carpet. A robot that vacuumed when activated from reception. He lived under the bed when not in use. I named him Stanley.

Diane and Hector returned to me on their tenth wedding anniversary, just as I had hoped. When they entered the room, I was confused. There was no child in sight. I presumed they must have left their offspring at home, perhaps with Diane's mother, so they could enjoy a break. But it quickly became apparent their conception efforts two years prior had not borne fruit. Also, they were not alone. Another couple stood beside them.

'This is much better than last time,' Hector said, inspecting my updated features.

'It's been getting great reviews,' said Diane. 'What do you guys think?'

The new woman flopped down on the bed. 'Fantastic. Plenty of room for all of us in here, eh?'

All four laughed a little nervously.

The new couple was called Federica and Sebastian. They were approximately the same age as Diane and Hector, although their demeanour was more carefree.

Federica sat up and pulled the dress she was wearing over her head. She unclipped her bra and pushed her underwear down to her ankles, stepping out of it as she stood up. She strode confidently past Sebastian, Hector and Diane to the window, where she stretched, arms raised high above her head, body twisting as she worked out the kinks in her shoulders.

'Someone's keen,' Hector said, glancing at his wife.

'You know what she's like,' said Sebastian. 'Any excuse will do.'

'It's nothing you haven't seen before,' Federica said, as she raised her right leg, placing the sole of her foot against the opposite thigh in a yoga pose. 'Besides, who wears clothes in hotel rooms? Diane, honey, can you support me while I do a back bend?'

'Sure thing,' Diane said, shrugging and turning her palms up to Hector as if to say, *'Oh well, here we go.'* She undressed and joined Federica by the window.

The men watched as the naked women bent and stretched together.

'You think people can see in from that office building?' Sebastian asked.

'Let's hope so,' Hector said. 'Brighten someone's day.'

Hector placed his hand on the back of Sebastian's neck and gripped his hair between his fingers, pulling the man in for a kiss. They removed each other's clothes and Sebastian took Hector's cock in his mouth. The women stopped stretching and approached the bed, hand in hand, to observe. An inventive and breathless ninety minutes ensued.

After, four bodies lay entwined on my bed. Eight eyes stared up at my ceiling.

Federica ducked her chin to sniff her armpit. 'Oof. I need a shower,' she said.

'I like how you smell when you sweat,' said Hector.

'Like fried onions,' said Sebastian.

'Let me have a sniff,' said Diane.

Federica offered her raised arm.

Diane squirmed in close, one arm draped across Federica's breast, and took a deep breath. 'That makes me hungry,' she said, abruptly licking Federica's armpit.

Federica yelped and tried to shuffle away, but Sebastian penned her in on the other side.

Hector rose from the bed. 'We could order room service,' he said, as he retrieved the menu.

'Whoever delivers that's going to get a shock,' said Sebastian.

Diane laughed. 'It would be worth doing, just to see the look on their face.'

'Big deal,' said Federica, climbing out from between Sebastian and Diane to stand next to Hector and read the menu. 'A loving couple fucking another loving couple. So what?'

Diane idly traced the blond hairs on Sebastian's abdomen with her fingers.

'Probably happens more often than you think,' said Hector. 'I might order the tempeh burger.'

'I don't know that it does,' said Federica. 'But it should. A real shot in the arm for both our relationships, eh?'

'Who knew four was the ideal number?' said Sebastian, nuzzling Diane's neck.

'Order me the eggplant,' said Federica, slapping Hector on the arse. 'You guys want anything?'

'I think they're going to be occupied for a little while,' said Hector. 'They're getting back into it.'

Hector and Federica watched for a minute or two, then Hector ordered food. Federica casually cradled his balls as he talked on the phone.

'Christ,' he said, after hanging up. 'It really gets me going watching them.'

'So I see. Let's leave them to it. Come join me in the shower.'

This was not the first time I had witnessed such an arrangement, although Federica was correct. In the decade since meeting Hector and Diane, it had not occurred often. Jealousy and insecurity had proven to be insurmountable barriers.

Having donned robes for the sake of propriety when room service was delivered (an extra pair were hung in my closet prior to them checking in, which had made me wonder), the two couples lounged on the bed and couch amid the remnants of their meal.

'Shall I tell them?' Federica asked Sebastian, who was finishing the last of his Thai beef salad.

'Might as well get it over with,' said Sebastian.

'What?' said Diane. 'You guys aren't breaking up with us, are you?'

'God, no,' said Federica, sitting on the end of the desk to face the couple on the couch. 'We plan on being with you two for a long time.'

'Besides, Ali adores you,' Sebastian added. 'Having a second mother and father is honestly ideal. Raised by the village, and all that.'

'He's the sweetest kid.' Hector put his arm around Diane. 'He's been great for us, given our situation.'

'About that,' said Federica, taking a deep breath. 'How would you guys feel about having a baby together?'

'How would that work?' said Diane.

'It already has.' Federica opened her robe and tapped her belly. 'I'm pregnant.'

This news hung in the air for ten silent seconds.

'Which one of us is the father?' Hector asked quietly.

Federica shrugged. 'No way of knowing yet. Could be either of you. Could be both. It doesn't matter. We thought since we already have Ali, you could have this baby, and we'll back each other up.'

'Holy shit,' said Diane. 'Are you serious? You'd give us the baby?'

'Sure. We want to. If that's what you'd like.'

Diane's mouth opened and closed. She looked at Hector and burst into tears.

'Uh, is that a yes, or a no?' Federica asked.

'It's a yes,' Hector said, holding his wife. 'My God, thank you. This is, well, this is a beautiful and unexpected turn of events.'

'Not to dump too much on you at once,' said Sebastian. 'But from a practical perspective, I think we should also buy a place together when we get back. We'll need some space to raise our legion of ragamuffins.'

And so, on their tenth wedding anniversary, the lovers of Hector and Diane presented them with the ultimate gift. I like to believe that without me this would never have happened. The child did not have four parents. It had five.

If my interaction with Diane and Hector, and now Federica and Sebastian, had ended with that visit, I would not have been disappointed. I had already been privy to more of their lives than I could have hoped for. We are places of passage, of transience. We expect nothing from those who glide through us. I played my role and did something good with my time. Hector and Diane and Federica and Sebastian would live on, outside of me, apart from me, and I would never know what became of them. Eventually, I would be demolished, perhaps to make way for another hotel, or an apartment block, or nothing. The city around me would grow to a megalopolis and I would be lost in the clutter of streets, or it would perish, and I would become rubble, and then dust.

When Diane showed up just over a year later, I was pleasantly surprised to see her. She crept quietly into the room, pushing a stroller. She looked around and sighed deeply before lifting a baby from the pram.

'Hector would think I'm crazy for doing this, Seven-one-nine, but he's away with work, so he'll never know. I thought it would be nice to get out of the house for a night, give F and S some alone time with Ali. But mostly, I wanted you to see Cassandra. She's yours, in a way. I'm sure you must feel that. So, here she is. Here's our daughter.'

Diane held the baby aloft and walked around me, unsure where my eyes might be. The child gurgled and laughed. Her fists opened and closed, as if gripping something insubstantial. Concentrating, I wrapped myself around her. For a moment – a fleeting second – it felt real.

KISS TOMORROW GOODBYE

when its night its safer to go thru tunnels unless it rains and then you cant go in cos the floodwaters come and wash everything away the only creatures that survive is crawfish and black widder spiders I seen them baby widders coming outta white eggs there was a big nest in a pipe with hunderds of them all shiny and tiny and fast Carrie got bit once on the finger and it swole up all red and pus came out and she had to go to the clinnik for a shot but she was

hot tonight and no rain for weeks so its a good time for a shortcut to Blue Fountain cept its dark and my torch doesnt have no battrys left but I know the way just stay in the middle tunnel till you come to Devons camp hes not there probs dumpster diving or collecting credits from the poker machines that tourists left behind Devons funny I like him espesh when he puts on that old suit and tries to look fancy so they wont throw him out of Flamingo dont think they know he lives right below them dont think anyone knows he said his mom hired a man to find him one time and the man found him sure nuff cos he was busted for smashing the winder of the Sev after they tried to charge him for ice even tho hed been going there for ages and getting it for free his mom come down below to visit him and cried and told him to come home but Devon said no hes forty-three and can look after himself but she gave him clean socks and underwear cept he dont wear none so he gave me a pair that was too big but I liked them so I cut the top open and put a string thru and pulled it tight like a belt it was funny and all the smurfs in Blue Fountain laughed and

stop and rest for a bit on Devons foldy chair hes got some real useful stuff like coat hangers theys good for making wind chimes or alarms so you hear if strangers is sneaking up on your camp hes got a big bag of plastic bottles too tut tut Devon you should know better thems worth a lot of money probs gonna take them to resyk but shouldnt leave them lying round like that untended case a troll or goblin comes and takes them gobs need cash dollars sos they can buy meth maybe I better stay here for a bit and guard them for Devon cept I dont have nothing for defence not even a knife just spells and magik but maybe gobs aint heard them yet not everyone knows but they will soon nuff

dont like wearing boots its not natral if you dont walk on barefoot then youre not connected to earth cept in tunnels youve got to have boots cos theres broken glass and hypodemic nerdles and maybe snakes or crockerdiles that nip your ankles tho I never seen none of those waters almost up to my knees in the channel where I have to go and the roofs low so I gotta crouch and it hurts my neck but this is the best way home theres light up ahead shining down thru the grate I can hear cars and taxis roaring up above and people talking and phones beep beeping and music sounds but then it passes mustve been coming from someones Cadillac Escalade ESV six point two litre eight speed transmission with surround view camera and 5G connectivity that I seen in the catalog Carrie brung to Blue Fountain they come in all kinds of funny colours like Black Raven and White Diamond and Majestic Plum and Shale with Cocoa Accents but mine would be Red Passion Tintcoat red for blood

tunnel comes out near the gallery lots of pictures there my favourites the giant ant tags and big statements bout art Cagney makes heard he was famous but nobody ever sees him cept I seen him lots of times and I always says hello cos thats how I was brung up polite like *hey JKa* he says to me *where you going this time of night* going fishin I says catch me some of them crawfish cos theys huge way bigger than back home *maybe theyre mutants* he says *you sure its okay to eat them* course I says eaten them a million times never done me no harm here mind my stuff while I go swimming will you *sure okay* he says looking at me funny while I take my clothes off *you want me to cover my eyes* he says and I says back what for dont care who sees me dont matter perfectly natral wouldnt never wear clothes if didnt have to *okay cool* he says guarding my stuff while I catch fishies Cagneys used to being on guard Metro been after him since he done that big graff on Tropicana nobody knows how he did it must have pretended to be cleaning winders and used special paint that only showed up at night Cagney was long gone by then but everyone saw what he wrote for weeks *kiss tomorrow goodbye* with big beautiful lips in my favourite colour red maybe he might draw me sometime and Ill be famous up there in lights

security guard tonight is Wayne hes okay not mean like some who ask smurfs to do stuff so they wont tell whos living in Blue Fountain worst is Jason Argonauts he always comes to Blue Fountain and picks a girl smurf for sucky sploshy asked me one time but only one time cos I dont do sexy stuff but he didnt know that so I just grind my teeth and make sounds like Im eating his thing like a sausage and he says *forget it no way you need a shower girl youre cray cray* not bothered dont care what Jason Argonauts thinks I knows things he doesnt know if he did know his head would splode maybe mine did but its still on my shoulders always had a good head on my shoulders thats what Momma said good for brainboxing and thinking fast so fast cant keep up where was I oh yeah hi Wayne you coming to next rave party no guess not have to protect our secret lair from Metro and Clark County rezoning commission

there she is waiting for me to get home my little kitty Zariella yes look I brung you a fishy scooped up in my pocket your favourite num num nums youre fatter than me kitty you been eating mice and lizards all day pest control thats why your smurf friends love you and you been keeping my bed warm good girl Zariella you in your natral habitat here aint that right kitties is desert animals and youre the colour of sand so you blend right in cammerfladge them rats dont even see you coming you like to sit on them dead critters and get all stinky dont you yes you do yes you do Zariella little lion of God come here and rub that stink on me and lets have a bath tomorrow or next day or one after

late night all quiet in Blue Fountain but Im awake and hear the signal Zariella hears it too and goes off running probs just Carrie she always comes home last I got the watchtower this week so its my turn to operate the lift *Jess Jess its me* hisses Carrie *throw down the rope* yeah yeah hold your horses I says my torch is out of battrys and I cant see for shit *dont fall* she goes *watch the edge* I know I know done this a million times she shines her torch right up in my eyes and laughs *there she is* she says *the naked gatekeeper* its hot I says and I need to do laundry Carrie shakes her head as I send the rope down *I like how you dont care* she says *dont ever change Jess theres too many people hung up on their body dysmorphia* say what now I goes honestly half of what Carrie says goes whoosh right over my head put your foot in the loop I says and I pulls her up you got bricks in your pocket or what I says *nah just a bun in the oven remember* oh yeah still tiny tho right *like a chicken egg* she goes *not showing yet not time to hatch come here and give me a hug* jeez youre in a good mood I says knowing she probs hooked up with Jackson again hes okay not great just okay but he wont hang round once her baby chicken comes clucking out *oh my God* she says stepping back her face all scrunched up *I love you and all JKa but seriously it must be time for your weekly bath* yeah yeah dont nag Im going tomorrow *wow you are ripe pungent foxy* shut up I says how come the cat doesnt complain *maybe* Carrie says *maybe because she already smells of dead rat* yeah thanks for that youre a real pal

when I says bath time for all smurfs Marco jumps to it cos he knows he gets to see me with no clothes Marco skates and hes smart not college big word clever like Carrie but everyday smarts plus he likes getting tickled espesh by me Carrie says hes got a crush on me so he watches me at bath time cept it must be the millionth time so whats the big deal think hed be used to it by now but no spose Marco keeps doing what I say till I tickle his splishy sploshy anyways time to clean my nooks and crannies ladies go first in the big tub *thats gender normative behaviour* Carrie says *reinforcing traditional stereotypes of women as the weaker sex* then I goes you really want to get in that water after Marco and all the boy smurfs *fair point* she says *Im willing to set aside my feminist principles this one time rather than bathe in their bacterial soup who knows what we might catch* logic and reason wins in the end

not sure how it works but Marco says the pipes inside the compost keep the water warm espesh in the sun even tho its stinky we dont need no lectrics in Blue Fountain long as weve got sunshine I got a mini foldy solar charger sos I can power up my pod and listen to sick beats doof doof doof doof me and Carrie and Rube and Rubes friend Lady Panorama all climb in together and splash and scrub and wash each others backs and fronts and between toes Lady Panoramas not technically a girl she still has her splishy sploshy but shes saving up so her tail matches her top got some nice pointy titties bit like mine and takes her pills reglar so shes more woman than all of us

unespected visitors to Blue Fountain always causes a crisis thats why Carrie bursts into my room whats with you I says and by the way you ever hear of knocking I couldve been whizzing in my bucket or anything *seen you piss a thousand times* she goes *theres some boy downstairs says he knows you* what the frig I says *you better come and sort this out* she goes *Im not happy Jess you cant be inviting whoever you want to come here not without consulting the committee* cool your jets I says everythings politicks with you Carrie I never invited nobody *well hes asking for you so you better come* right okay let me eyeball the guy afore you start throwing things at him dont forget our pact of no violence *dont lecture me* she goes *Im the one wrote the manifesto and theres a clear mandate for resorting to physical force as a last resort if the collective is threatened by outsiders* okay okay I says and I follows her down the stairs to the first floor and shouts who goes there *JKa its me* says a boys voice I werent sure who it was at first and I couldnt see him cos he was standing under the watchtower who is that I goes whats your name *yeah identify yourself* shouts Carrie *who the fuck are you* the boy steps out and I see hes got a grey hoodie on and baggy jeans dirty sneakers must be boiling in that get up *its me* he says and I was wondering why he wouldnt say his name till I saw it was Cagney nobody knows his real name anyways and I knowed if I said who he was Carrie wouldnt believe me and she would never let him come up so I says hey buddy havent seen you in daylight afore whats up *you know him* Carrie goes course I says hes a friend of mine I see in the tunnels sometimes *well who is he then* listen Carrie I goes getting right annoyed youre not in charge round here youre not the boss of me so quit it with the aggro its none of your beeswax who he is hes a friend of mine and thats all you need to know I dont go round questioning who you hang out with do I *Im just looking after the best interests of the community* she goes no youre not I says youre so caught up in your frigging self that you forget to be nice and not mean to everyone so piss off for once and quit sticking your nose into other peoples business not everyones involved in a spiracy to repress you *how dare you speak to me like that* she goes *Im going to convene a meeting of the committee later to talk about this* fine do what you like I says now get out of the way Im bringing my friend up and off she goes cursing and complaining honestly what a drama queen thought my brainbox was broke but maybe Im not so bad after all

sorry bout the mess I says dont usually get many guests *its okay* he goes *do you mind if I sit down Im exhausted* no problemo I says brushing stuff off my mattress Zariella jumps out the way but she doesnt run like usual instead she hangs round to sniff Cagneys foot must smell good to her maybe smells like dead rat he looks like hes been sleeping in the tunnels for a while in fact he looks pretty bad you okay brother I ask him you been knocked round a bit here let me get you some water and some grub he eats fast so I know hes hungry poor kid probs younger than me but its hard to tell hes so dirty and banged up *God thats good* he says *thanks JKa Im so sorry for fronting up like this but I didnt know where else to go* what happened I says not believing how Zariellas snuggling gainst him and trying to get on his lap usually shes spicious of strangers *hey little one* he goes rubbing her ears and she turns the motor on Cagney just strokes her for a bit and looks like hes gonna cry *shit JKa* he says *I really appreciate this I thought I was a goner there before I remembered where you lived* yeah bout that I says I never brung you here so who told you where I live the residents of Blue Fountain dont take kindly to strangers cos we try to keep this place secret otherwise we could get kicked out *sorry sorry* he says looking guilty *I followed you one night because I was curious to see where you crashed its amazing this place totally smart of you guys to squat here hope Im not causing you any problems* dont sweat it I says Ill deal with Carrie and her committee we all think its a joke anyways *okay good* he says *I just need to sit for a bit* stay as long as you like I goes you on the run *that about sums it up* he says *I was graffing out the back of a gym and this big guy appears and knocks me off the dumpster didnt see him coming then he lays into me think he mightve broken a rib but I got away and ran into the storm drain he didnt follow I suppose he was scared the tunnel was full of cobwebs* you didnt get nipped by a black widder did you I asks *no I dont think so* he says oh youd know if you did I tells him so you must be sweet *okay good anyway Ive been stuck in there for maybe sixteen hours I got lost since it wasnt a tunnel system I recognised and I left my paint and torch and that back at the dumpster that fat motherfucker probably took it all* he says *eventually I found my way to the gallery where I did the giant ant painting* ooh I love that one thats my favourite I says *yeah thanks* he goes *and from there I knew how to get here it was a bit of a gamble but Ive run out of places to hide Metros on my ass bad these days theyre really making an effort to catch me* dont worry brother I says you can stay here with me and Zariella until youre feeling better Metro dont come round here cos we got private security in our pocket next thing he starts bawling and I had to find him a clean tissue and that werent easy let me tell you

weird having someone else sleeping in your bed but poor Cagney done passed out on me after he was finished sniffling I think he was at his wits end with all the stress of running from Metro and bad people trying to stop him from being an artist he probs hadnt slept in days so I laid him down and put a blankie over him plus Zariella curled up in his arms like she known him for years Ive never had much truck with boys but now Cagneys sleeping I can eyeball him real good got longish hair nice lashes and little soft wispy hairs on his lip and couple long ones on his chin but not a big beard like the nice guy who gives me free coffee at Cortez theres lots of nice peoples in Neon City trying to look after us strays probs cos theys only one patch of bad luck away from joining us thats how come most smurfs is in Blue Fountain just rotten luck shitty parents no jobs no money houses too spensive or whatevs Carrie says wes like characters from a novel by Charles Dickens she gived me one of his stories once Tale of Two Cities it were called pretty good one bout the Frenchies liked the starts was the best of times was the worst of times identerfied with that didnt finish it tho too much politicking anyways watching Cagney dozing is sending me off too maybe Ill stretch out next to him sure he wont mind since its my bed better keep clothes on tho dont want him getting funny ideas Carrie says boys cant be trusted spose she would know getting preggers and all must be weird feeling nother creature inside your belly crawling round and playing soccer with your guts maybe Ill never know

sunsets the bestest time to climb up to eagles nest even tho its a long way and hard work sore on the legs but plenty of spots to sit for a bit and rest Cagney feels better now hes had a sleep bit embarrassed bout his crying but thats okay I told him dont worry bout that everybody cries its natral and theres so much to cry bout in Neon City not for me persnly Im not worried bout nothing no more *thanks for not telling anyone who I am* Cagney goes as we walks up the endless stairs *the less people who know the better* its alright I says everyone thinks Im cray cray anyhows and probs wouldnt believe me even if I had Justin Beebers in my bed *thats why I trust you JKa* Cagney says *you always tell the truth the problem is most people dont want to hear it when it makes them uncomfortable* maybe I should take you with me next time I see my case worker I tells him so you can splain to her bout all the truth bombs I been dropping *you have a case worker* he says all sprised sure shes not a bad lady bit of a pain cos she always asks questions bout where Im staying and who Im hanging round with and she tries to give me pills but I just sells them dont wanna get zonked Momma said theres nothing wrong with me Im just a fast thinker like Speedy Gonzales andale andale arriba arriba *dont take any pills they give you youre way better like this* Cagney says *shit how much farther is it JKa Im whacked already* only nother twenty floors I goes you got to get way up the top for the view dont worry theres supplies up there and a bed we can stay the night and come down in the morning its Rubes turn as watcher so

I can do what I likes plus its private nobody bothering us got my pod in my pack so we can dance maybe even have a secret rave and I brung some paints so you can make a graff *no way you did not* yeah I did knowed youd want to make art cept you lost your cans so I brung mine *youre a legend* he says better get on I says dont want to miss the sunset its spectakler

nearly there now not far *youve been saying that the last fifteen minutes* Cagney goes right I says cept every time its truer and truer so whats the biggie Cagney just shakes his head *you mentioned your momma before* he goes *is she still around* ah here we go I shouldve known this was coming walked right into it really for mentioning her at all its complicated I says *hey no problem if you dont want to talk about it thats alright I respect that my mom was no great shakes either* its not that I dont like her I goes its just that shes in a bad place and talking bout it aint gonna help her none plus I cant visit her cos theyd take one look at me and tie me to the bed next to her Cagney stops to catch his breath and says *is she committed* hey wes all committed I goes youre committed to graffing all over public buildings to make statements bout art and thats why youre famous all over the world and Carries committed to her politicks even tho shes mean bout it sometimes *let me ask you this* Cagney goes *you dont have to answer if you dont want to but how in holy fuck did you wind up living in an abandoned casino complex in Las Vegas JKa* okay well thats the big question aint it Cagney and you just go right ahead and ask *look if its a secret thats okay* he goes *you dont have to tell me shit but you already know one of my secrets JKa youre one of the only people in the world who knows who I really am so you can trust me* lets get to the top I says cos itll be right annoying if weve done all this climbing for nothing last one ups a rotten egg

you werent kidding were you Cagney says as we look out the winders of eagles nest at the sun setting over Neon City how piktureskew is that I goes or is it pikachu I always get them mixed up *its picturesque but never mind I like the way you say it better* Cagney says *what an amazing view you can see all the way out to the desert* we watch the sun setting behind the strip and all the lights blinking on in Neon City like the spaceport from Star Wars then we sits down to eat a can of peaches *you have to tell me how you wound up here* Cagney goes I lick my fingers and gets myself comfy on the mattress not sure who was here last but it dont smell too bad mustve taken ages dragging it all the way up them stairs right I goes its a pretty mazing story and all true I swears but you has to let me tell it and dont be interrupting even if you has questions or needs clarryfickation *dont worry Im a good listener* Cagney says then are you ready you look ready okay lets begin

once pon a time long time ago in a land far far way well maybe not that far not sure sactly how far to be honest still in Merica land of the free home of the brave but not here in Neon City somewhere else I member there was a river and trees and a dirt track there was a lady called Momma and her baby girl JKa now she probs had a daddy cept cant say for sure cos he never come round with presents or to teach JKa how to ride a bisikle had to learn that one herself trial and error near broke her neck once when the handybars popped out after jumping over some stingy nettles crashed real bad that time Momma said what dont hurt you makes you stronger anyways werent easy living in the forest Momma had a job in town couple days a week serving eggs and bacons to men who came thru in trucks sometimes one stopped by the house to say hello and JKa always asked if they knowed her daddy but they never did JKa spent plenty of time on her ownsome learning how to do things and fending for herself caught up in her head thinking and imagining adventures with magikal friends she had lots of them cept nobody else could see them then one night Momma and JKa was home together and it was dark and raining real hard cold so they was snuggled up next to the fire when Momma hears a noise and tells JKa to stay put while she vestigates it were lights strange lights in the trees getting brighter and brighter till JKa was blinded couldnt see nothing then big flash and everything goes white and dont member what happened next cept when JKa wakes up next to Momma theys in a cold room and got no clothes on Mommas got bloods on her face and legs shivering scared bloods on me too cept dont member how it got there whats happening Momma where are we JKa says *listen baby* Momma goes *were in trouble wes been abducted* is that good or bad JKa asks not knowing for sure *its bad* Momma says *real bad* who is it done the abducktin JKa wonders is it aliens Momma spacemen from nother planet *yes baby* Momma says *yes thats right thats who it is they come for us and were not on Earth anymore honey wes on another world just think of it like that thats better* oh cool JKa says what do they look like the aliens is they tall and slender and has big eyes *yes yes* Momma says *just like that* and shes crying a bit cos shes sore JKas not sore dont feel nothing at all just cold Momma why is there bloods on us JKa asks its all icky but Momma just looks all sad and goes *its cos aliens probed us baby Im sorry they probed us looked inside of us and it hurts it hurts but dont worry youll be okay* I am okay Momma JKa tells her if they did that to me dont member *good good* she says *thats for the best I wish I could forget* Momma tells her *listen baby I have a plan to get us out of here* oh wow JKa goes are we gonna steal one of their spaceships Momma howd you even know how to fly one that makes Momma smile nice to see her happy she dont smile much cept when she gets good tips and brings home cake *heres what were gonna do* she says *when next one of them aliens comes in Mommas gonna distract him so you can run now thing is JKa wes not on Earth member so the gravitys different which means you can run real fast much faster than normal and maybe jump too so soon as that door opens and you see a way out I want you to run baby you run and dont stop till you get back to Earth and find someone to tell bout the spaceship* what bout you Momma JKa goes how you gonna get away *Im not Jessika* Momma says *but you are and thats all that matters you promise me you wont look back just keep running* okay momma dont worry JKa tells her I can run real fast espesh if gravity helps me *one more thing baby* Momma says crying lots now *member how I told you that the parts tween your legs is where babies come out of well they dont work no more cos the aliens took them away but youre special youre so so special my beautiful girl so dont let no one touch you there again okay theres no point theres nothing left* okay Momma I says thats alright dont unerstand how babies grow up there dont make no sense never believed it anyways then an alien with big round eyes and pale skin came in and Momma done her bit to distract him and JKa scoots out the door past his legs he tried to grab her but she was too quick down the corridors of his spaceship she went bouncing along using the gravitys and out a porthole held her breath cos no air in space floated down to Earth and landed in bushes ouch sharp bits cut JKa but she rolled onto her feet and run into a forest them aliens was chasing her with bright lights but she hid and they didnt find her then day comes and JKa walks right out of there easy peasy lemon squeezy a family picked her up and gave her a blankie and took her to nice doctors that looked at bloods and kept some what they called ever dense anyways JKa stayed with the nice family for a while till Momma came back JKa went to visit her in hospital but she couldnt talk or nothing probs from speriments aliens did on her when Momma finally did talk she was all chatty and telling sheriffs and others bout being abduckted and how scary it was in the spaceship Mommas eyes were funny and doctors said something was wrong with her brainbox too much sycherlogikle traumer couldnt live with JKa no more but had to stay in special hospital for special people JKa visited for years and years then special hospital closed down and Momma was outside but nice new family couldnt take her no room not much moneys neither cos pop lost his job couldnt figure out where he left it never found it again JKa tried to see Momma but she was living in a box under a bridge down by the river like a troll didnt always rekernise JKa then one day she says shes going to Nevada cos aliens sposed to live there and she wants to ask them why they done speriments to her JKa waited till she was old nuff then went to find Momma and did find her but she was in nother hospital last time JKa seen her she was raving bout aliens coming back for her to take her to a moon far far away where aliens lived or used to live anyways theyre coming back for all of us who believes to take us to their moon and itll be home for everybody and Momma and JKa will finally be together again just like afore they was abduckted

have to be careful up in eagles nest once the sun goes down you can see for miles and miles but also people can see you so only candles for light its nice tho a bit spooky just cant set fire to the place its a big bored room or something where important men in suits sposed to meet and smoke cigars and decide on world future lots of space for dancing and scooting round found one of Marcos old decks with the wheels still working Cagney shows me some moves hes a pretty good skater Im not bad myself more of a cruiser than a trickster so just go round and round cant do ollies or nothing like Cagney *it feels like the world ended and we are the only survivors* he says safe from zombies I goes cant see them climbing all those stairs *listen* Cagney says *I been thinking JKa maybe I could do a painting of you on the wall here its crying out to be graffed on look how bare and inviting it is* oh you want to draw me thats so cool I was hoping you might *I was thinking* he goes *if you dont mind and if its not a trigger for you or anything of drawing you getting beamed up into a spaceship a flying saucer or something kind of like those old movies how would you feel about that is that weird I dont want to upset you* no way I says that wouldnt upset me at all why would that upset me thats pretty much sactly what happened when I was a kiddlywink and I hope thats whats gonna happen again when the aliens comes back to take me home what do you need from me Cagney stares at me for a bit as I scoot round on Marcos old deck think the story I told bout little JKa made him sad but oh well life goes on have to keep moving forward no point in looking back I always say nostalger aint my thang more excited bout the future than anything else *I don't need much* Cagney says *just pose for a bit with your arms up like youre being claimed by the light wont take long for me to get the outline down and then you can watch me do the rest* cool I says no problemo my pleasure let me fire up the pod sos we got a soundtrack Ill put on some space music theres this German DJ with lots of space sounds like waow waow pchew pchew in the background thatll get me in the mood here we go how does that sound pretty good eh *perfect* Cagney goes *now maybe we can make a circle from the candles and you can stand in the middle that way youll be lit from below its not ideal but Ill reverse the shadows* okay good *oh whoa hey no need to strip I can draw you as you are* nah I says better if Is nakids aint it thats how people gets drawed you seen my butt cheeks afore so no big deal *umm okay if thats what you prefer* Cagney goes *but so you know its not necessary* its done now I says we already knows each others secrets not like it matters anyways cos Momma said my sex parts dont work no more member *yeah yeah okay* Cagney says *umm so if you could stand in the circle of light okay wow yeah actually that looks great youre right much better with bare skin* I sniffs my armpit just to check Cagney laughs *you alright there* he goes oh yeah just making sure Im not too stinky dont want you passing out or nothing lucky for you I had a bath this morning *you probably smell better than I do* he says *Im the one who spent the night crawling around in the storm drains* okay so if I stand like this with my arms up how does that look *perfect just perfect stay like that for a minute and dont move let me work my magic* such a good feeling standing there arms up all natral not caring and being drawed I feels powerful and strong and ready for anything put my head back close my eyes and Im gone gone all the way gone

mazing so mazing cant believe its me up there look look wish there was lots of peoples here to see it cant wait till other smurfs comes up oh Cagney I love it its so good so so good youre so talented cant believe it thank you thank you so much for drawing me making me famous cmere I says cmere you needs all the hugs in the world all the hugs I got to give *okay okay* he goes *take it easy you got no clothes on remember* dont care I says want to wrap myself round you and hug you till you cant breathe plant kisses all over your neck and face mwah mwah mwah *yeah dont JKa dont sorry you better stop that and get off me* okay I tells him Im just happy so happy woo think its time to dance hey dance with me at least *alright* Cagney laughs *I can dance sure but dont you want to get dressed first* nah no way whats the point I says only get my clothes all sweaty and I just done laundry this morning past the point of no return now

wake up pretty dark bit cold have to pull blankie round me was snuggling up to Cagney holding on tight arms wrapped round him from behind he kept clothes on cos hes shy I didnt bother with clothes cos its warmer that way slept pretty good after dancing for ages and laughing and talking bout how Cagney growed up in a small town *nice place bit boring* he said *mom and dad still kicking on out there* he keeps in touch tells them hes working always moving tho so they dont get funny ideas bout coming to visit feels a bit bad they dont know the truth but itd freak them out so better this way being a rebel drifter famous graffer anyways where is Cagney he was here a minute ago stretch and yawn hope he hasnt fallen down the stairs or something pretty dark up here in eagles nest cant hardly see nothing with candles out just stars and moon sliver better go find him see if hes alright probs gone to use the bucket in the room where toilets sposed to be bit ew but no choice either that or pee out the winder better check make sure he can find his way back in the dark yep hes in there alright can hear him whizzing pretty loud in that bucket gonna leap out and surprise him ha ha sneak up real quiet and BOO scared ya *Christ you almost gave me a heart attack* he goes why you doing poops in middle of night Cagney mustve been them peaches *no no Im just tinkling* he says *can I get some privacy please* right I goes cept heres the thing if youre just whizzing why you sitting down Cagney never seen a boy do that afore your aim pretty bad or something *ah shit* he goes shaking his head and then he finishes whizzing gives a little wipe with toilet paper and stands up pants round his ankles cept cant see his splishy sploshy so maybe its more a case of her ankles ha ha I says whod a thunk it Cagneys a girl

let me get this straight I says are you a boy turning into a girl like Lady Panorama or a boy born with lady parts or what *no just a plain old girl* Cagney goes *Ive been pretending to be a boy for a long time now so long I sometimes forget who and what I really am I mean it helps that Ive always looked boyish and then when I started graffing it made sense cos the work I do sometimes takes me into dangerous places places where its better to be a man or at least places where youd be treated different if you were a woman basically it was a question of personal safety but then the whole Cagney identity began to form and I was kind of stuck with it which made me realise it was a golden opportunity to pull the wool over everyones eyes especially once I started doing big pieces on public buildings that attracted interest from Metro and the media and the art world everyone wants to know who Cagney is and I kind of like how they have absolutely no idea that its some girl from Poughkeepsie I suppose it will all come out some day probably when I get caught but thatll be funny too seeing peoples reactions anyway sorry for keeping you in the dark JKa Im kinda used to hoodwinking people but now youre in the inner circle* wow I goes how many other people know *well its a small circle* he says I mean she says what am I sposed to call you I goes *not much point in keeping up the pretence when its just the two of us* she says *look my real names Charmaine but the only people who call me that are my mom and dad still if you want to use it go ahead just be careful who you say it in front of* okay dont worry bout Carrie and the smurfs I says could be better if I calls you Charmaine rather than Cagney theys less likely to question that plus Carries all for more girls joining the collective so ironicly youd be hiding out here under your real identity *its been handy* she says *saved my ass a couple times when I had to get in somewhere just dress like a girl and you get waved right in* hard to imagine you dressing like a girl I says anyways you coming back to bed Im cold *oh sure* she says *just give me a minute Ill be right there*

is this weird I feel weird please tell me if this is weird no I says dont be silly stop standing there shivering with no clothes on and get under this blankie Ill warm you up *I just wanted you to see I wasnt lying* she goes *believe me Im not very comfortable being naked in front of someone I spend so much time hiding my body that its always a shock when Im exposed* nuff chitter chatter I says get in here girl its all settled youre a woman I can see that no dangling splishy sploshy youre all good *thanks* she says squirming in next to me *my clothes were pretty smelly anyway I really need to wash them sorry I probably need a shower too cleaned up the best I could* who cares bout that I says pulling her in tight skin on skin thats better be toasty in a minute put my arms round her front and squeeze *Jesus* she goes breathing all funny *Jesus its been a while God that feels good umm you can warm your hands on my breasts if you want JKa only if you want* no need to tell me twice I grabs a handful nice and warm want me to squeeze em and play with your nips I goes thats fun Lady Panorama done that to me this morning when we was in the bathtub she plays with all the girl smurfs titties think its cos shes obsessed with woman stuff *oh* Cagney goes *hmm yeah thats quite good you can play with them as much as you like* fine sure no probs I goes nice and squishy must be tricky keeping these kittens under wraps eh *can I touch yours* she says totes I goes lets swap positions you get behind me that way you get the warmth too come on get a handful theys different from yours more pointy *hmm* she goes breathing on my neck lips touching giving me little tickly kisses hey I says listen Cag I mean Charmaine Im happy to fool round and stuff no probs there done that afore with boys let em kiss me and touch my titties and played with their splishy sploshy but you have to member I aint got no sex parts so maybe not much fun for girls cos I know they likes to play with each others down below bits Carrie says its good better than what boys does but cant really unerstand it persnly anyways just so you know *hmm* she says *hmm* dont know that shes paying much attenshun seems pretty busy kissing and licking my neck and ears and squeezing my nips pushing gainst me can feel her down below hairs gainst my butt then she does a funny thing werent specting it tickles my tummy and below hairs then touches me somewheres under and I goes whoa shitballs what was that and pulls her hand away *its okay JKa* she says whispering in my ear *let me show you* and then I goes hmm and oh and aah and ooh and ay yi yi andale andale arriba arriba

lose a day a whole day not sure where we put it hanging out in eagles nest eating foods and drawing and running round nakids and sploring each others bodies Charmaine shows me where to touch and splained how it works I get it now duh who needs a squirty boy splishy sploshy when you got girl parts much better neat and tidy and just press the button and kablam Charmaine shows me how to use your tongue ooh thats the bestest she can do that to me all day and she does do it all day tween sleeps and cans of peaches and me doing it to her course Im a quick learner and like the noises she makes when I lick her real soft then side to side then make the number eight over and over eight plus eight plus eight plus eight equals pop goes the weasel only fight we had was bout my sex parts and whether they was still there not the outer bits but whats inside way up in there the place where babies get made Charmaine says I still got them and that they werent took away by nobody that was just a story Momma told sos to protect me sos I wouldnt get preggers Charmaines pretty smart but I had to disagree with her on this persnl matter cos I knows for sure that the aliens took my babymaker they whisked it right out of me aint nothing up there cept spiderwebs and a little empty cave maybe with some old homeless dude rolled up in a sleeping bag dont wake him Charmaine says Im crazy which I knowed already but crazy in a funny way *what about your monthlies how do you explain those* she goes dont have to splain them I says dont got none *what are you talking about* she goes *you get your period right* nope I says nothing happening no bloods or nothing aint never had them bit of a blessing really if you ask me and Charmaine looks real concerned *you ever seen a doctor about it* she asks course I says when I scaped from the spaceship doctors looked all over me and in me and put things in my mouth and my butt and every hole I got you had a look yourself didnt you *well* she goes *I cant get that far inside you so I couldnt say for sure* take it from me I says Im all good nothing going on just wee comes out of there and thats it she looks sad then *maybe they did something to you damaged you in some way those bastards* its alright I goes least I still got the launch button

night again and wes all rested and feeling good been sleeping and loving each other all day so wide awake now what we gonna do Charmaine I says you want to head out *funny you should mention that* she goes *I was thinking the same thing how would you feel about working on a big project with me theres something Ive had my eye on for a while its risky so I need someone to keep lookout* you want me to keep peepers for you I says like while you do a graff *yeah and also to help carry my stuff I got a stash of paint in the tunnels plus you know the way down there so thatll work to our advantage* where we going I says *you know that mega church out on Summerlin Parkway the one that preaches gay people will go to hell Ive been meaning to pay them a visit for a while now I got a little surprise for them* oh yeah I says thats near the interstate theres a storm drain comes out not far from there bit of a hike but we got all night and Im not tired at all Charmaine what bout you *baby* she says *I could run all night with you by my side* aww thats sweet I says giving her kisses on the neck hey Charmaine I just thought are you one of the gay womens the lesbians I spose you must be since youre such an expert on the workings of lady sex parts but she just looks at me and laughs *come on* she says *lets get suited up its time to get into character*

tunnels is dark and scary at night but I knows the way thru the labyrinth and I brung plenty of spare battrys for the torches sos we dont get lost and trapped forever and have to live down here like gobs or trolls Cagney keeps hearing things critters I spose rats and fish and mutant ducks with scorpion stingers quack quack zap zap but dont worry I says JKa is a friend to animals cept the tasty ones none gonna hurt us she wants me to call her Cagney now not Charmaine she looks like a boy again thats some disguise sure fooled me we set out early cos its hours afore we come out the drain under the freeway still traffic zooming along but they cant see us wes ghosts ninjas assassins with backpacks of spray paint Cagney knows the way from here shes happy to be out in the open air even tho its a hot night whats the plan I says when wes crouching down near the mouth of the tunnel bit of garbage lying round an old shopping cart with wheels missing McDonalds cups a squished soccer ball but no peoples living here too noisy with the freeway upstairs *we take backstreets to the church* Cagney goes drawing a map in the dirt like in the movies cool I says should we shrinkernise our watches *I dont wear a watch* Cagney goes thats okay I tells her neither do I *so were gonna head round the back of the building* she says *theres some cover there from a low wall and we cant be seen from the road but it opens onto an alley and if a cruiser goes past theyll spot us straightaway were kinda exposed so youll have to keep your eyes open* no problemo I says you can depend on me Ill keep my peepers peeled and if any five oh rolls up Ill signal you and were outta there whats the signal by the way ooh can it be an owl I know how to do the owl hoot hoo hoo hoo *thats supposed to be an owl* Cagney goes course I says but if you dont like it I can always do a tropical bird like MAKAW MAKAW *shh* she says *Jesus keep your voice down we dont want to attract attention* oh yeah sorry guess itll have to be my lame ass owl then *okay okay* she says *the owls not that bad* cept what if a real owl comes along and makes the signal by accident I goes that could get confusing maybe I should do nother bird hey what bout a daktil theres none of them round no more so no chance of a mix up *were not doing a pterodactyl* Cagney says a bit sasperated *just stick to the frigging owl JKa* okay good owls are cool *right are you ready* yes Im ready *okay were just gonna walk up there like its no big deal just two friends out for an evening stroll not up to any nefarious deeds so try not to look suspicious* me spicious I says I been blending in all my life I can walk the streets of Neon City and aint nobody gonna even notice me I been training for this moment for years lead on Macduff *whered you hear that* Cagney says laughing dunno maybe one of them old fellers that lives in the tunnels maybe Devon hes always speaking in verse got quite the collection of books *alright JKa thats enough quiet now its game time* sorry I goes just excited okay poker face act natral just a couple of friends out for a harmless walk tra la la nothing to see here officer

have to push the dumpster up gainst the wall lucky it has wheels still heavy tho dont know what them Jesus creepers been throwing in the garbage Cagney rubs her palms together shes calm and in control now shes been here afore loads of times and knows how to get it done *oh man* she says *would you look at that wall just begging for it alright JKa boost me up then scooch down to the corner and make sure the coast is clear* dont sweat it I says I got your six its all quiet not a soul stirring cept the ones wandering round the church looking to get in cant see em of course but theys probly there outcasts rejects sinners the ones that didnt make it into heaven Gods a bit picky bout who he lets in no way Cagneys making it in not with her being a lesbians guess maybe me neither now I licked her widget still it was worth it Id do it again its natral for womens to touch each others parts Cagney starts drawing and I watch her for a bit afore she notices me staring and hisses *JKa youre supposed to be watching the corner get to your post* oopsie sorry Im on it just act natral have yourself a lean gainst the wall peekaboo down the street nothing that way nothing other way neither all good coast is clear shouldve come up with a signal to let Cags know its all good oh well guess no owl hoot is good news whats she drawing up there anyways hmm oh I see a body and white dress think she might be graffing a ghostie jeez she works fast guess shes used to it no time for fooling round *hows it looking* she asks mazing I goes *no not the graff the street are we clear* yeah yeah I says dead as a zombies eyes *okay good come up here a second will you I need to get on your shoulders* okey dokey I goes cept whos gonna be keeping watch *dont worry about that for now* she says *just have to risk it I cant reach the top* righto I says climbing up on the dumpster oof watch your foot just as well youre a slinky malinki hurry up will you *yeah yeah* she goes *I just gotta do the wings and the halo hold on a second* ah so its not a ghostie then *no* she says *its an angel doofus were desecrating a church here alright let me down thatll do no time for detail it doesnt matter anyway its all in the message jump down and help me move the dumpster again* jeez its hard work being your assistant I says *watch your tootsies one two three and push there we go now back to your post soldier* sir yes sir right away sir off I goes to the end of the alley to keep watch couple cars go past but nothing to worry bout just crawlers looking for action move along now move along hear a siren in the distance sounds like an ambulance probs someone started a fight in one of the casinos maybe stabby stabby or blam blam dont go in those places cos its life or death for them thats hooked on playing the bandits or pokers maybe someone took their life after losing big plenty of jumpers and overdoses and muskets to the temple casinos cover it all up dont want that getting out blood stains is bad for business *psst JKa hey girl get back here and tell me what you think of this* one last peek down the street all clear and back to the scene of the crime wow just wow theres Cagney stood back arms folded looking mighty satisfied with herself would you just look at that a huge angel cept with blood on its hands and red tears streaming down its cheeks plus the words in a big jagged scrawl *ANGELS WITH DIRTY FACES* clap my hands and jump up and down on the spot its so cool I says and them churchies aint gonna like it one bit probs wont last long theyll be out here with scrubby brushes tomorrow *better take a photo then* Cagney says and takes out a cute camera snaps a few and each time a little photo slides out the top oh thats neat I goes *this is the way it has to be* Cagney says *cant be taking digital photos in case I get hacked and they get traced back to me cant use a phone camera either or even a thirty-five mil unless you develop the shots yourself of course but its not like Ive got a dark room set up somewhere or anyone I can trust with this shit* its alright I says I unerstand the governments always watching got to be off the grid like us at Blue Fountain hey you better sign it sos they know who owned them *yep* she says shaking a can of white paint and doing her tag what a talent what a genius what a provockatoor Im feeling all gooey inside when I looks at her but then wes bathed in white light and for a second my heart leaps in my chest cos I think its the aliens come back to take me home but a booming voice goes *halt stay where you are* Cagney drops her spray can *fuck its Metro leg it JKa* she throws her backpack over her shoulder grabs me by the hand and we run the siren whoops and I hear the Metro cruiser zoom away from the end of the alley theys going round the corner to the front of the building to cut us off have to think smart and fast lucky thats how my brainbox works fast so fast I points to the resyk bin hop up onto that and over the wall Cagney right next to me like Bonnie and Clyde we is cept no wait Bonnie and Bonnie the two Bonnies Bonnie squared land in the alley hear the Metro cruiser screeching into the parking lot of the church theyll work out where we gone in a minute got to run to the end of the alley quick look into the street no backup cars not yet anyways sprint across and crouch down hide next to a Cadillac Escalade ESV six point two litre eight speed transmission with surround view camera and 5G connectivity parked outside shouldnt leave that out here untended theys the most stolen vehickles in Merica very nice up close tho just like the catalog says wait for the cruiser to pass spotlight searching they think we must be still in the alley but I got a plan ready Cagney I goes *yeah* she says *say the word* ready and go run across the main road lights on green this is the riskiest part cos if they shines their light down here were sprung Cagney starts laughing tho shes enjoying the thrill of the chase she grabs my hand raises it to her lips and kisses it as we charge down the next side street hear the siren whoop again but its not close hear the freeway too then run across the ramp woot woot nearly there and here comes Metro zooming up and screeching round the corner theys smarter than they looks but that aint saying much *stop stop immediately* their speaker voice goes oh sure like were gonna do that come get me if you can Cagney jumps down over the edge and Im right behind hear the tires squeal as Metro skids to a halt boots on the ground now probs six shooters drawn cowboys cept without the moral code just shoot you in the back like cowardy custards then wes back in the tunnels and sees torches flashing hears men shouting but we knows where wes headed and makes it to the mouth of madness the storm drain no way theyre following us in there not at night not even during the day theys scared of the darkness scared of the forgotten people and wes too fast too smart Cagney and JKa slip thru the cracks running keep running dont stop till we reach the shadows so black just like in space like the sky when you look up from the alien moon and then lickety split it swallows us up and were gone

AFTERWORD / ACKNOWLEDGEMENTS / BLAME APPORTIONED

The misconception about short stories is that because they're short they must be easy to write, or at least quick. Maybe they are for some people. I should be so lucky. This collection of nine stories, some of which aren't short at all, took ten years to write. One decade, from conception to publication. That's longer than *Mammoth*.

It's my own fault. I treated each of these stories as if they were novels. Exhaustive research, some involving travel to far-flung places. Interviews. Books bought, read and mulled over for years. Dozens of drafts. Hundreds of thousands of words written. Stories developed, written, rewritten and then discarded. I should've just gone to a café every afternoon for a month and banged out some mood pieces.

If you've reached this point in the book, you're probably thinking, what the hell was that all about? Where did these stories come from? Why did Flynn write them? What's wrong with him?

I owe you an explanation. So, here goes.

'Inheritance' has its genesis in a 2017 trip to Alaska to celebrate the ~~mid-life crisis~~ fiftieth birthday of Sarah, my writer pal/archenemy Nick Earls's wife, along with a bunch of their friends

I had never met, whom I assume he hired for the week. We stayed in the town of Girdwood, which is faithfully portrayed in the story, right down to the laundromat that sold Thai food and dope, the Mercantile general store and the tourists in puffer jackets (that was us). We saw bears, climbed a glacier and met a beautiful Russian spy who had infiltrated the Californian tech industry (hello, Julianna!). As writer leeches, Nick and I vacuumed up juicy details for potential future stories, and eventually came to a gentleman's agreement: we would share Girdwood. Thus, the town (and some of the characters here) also appear in his annoyingly good 2021 novel of linked stories, *Empires*.

In 2017, I was working for the RSPCA in Melbourne and seeing the world from an animal perspective, which made me ponder what it must be like for bears in that wild territory, having to put up with people being all outdoorsy every summer when they're trying to build up fat reserves for the big sleep. Naturally, I took the premise too far. 'Inheritance' clocks in at just under ten thousand words, but at one point it was closer to forty thousand. Knowing my publisher, Aviva Tuffield, and editor, Felicity Dunning, might spontaneously combust if I handed that in, I cut the story down to twenty thousand, which still pushed the boundaries of friendships and professional relationships. After much cajoling, arguing, pointing of fingers, levelling of accusations, title changes and legal challenges, we are content with this eighty-seventh draft version. If you want to see the actual bear from this story, look on my Instagram (@flythefalcon). I was way too close when I took that photo and am fortunate to be here today. And if you want to read more on theories of inherited memory, set aside six months and get ready to step through the looking glass.

—

'22F' began percolating after watching the 1998 Werner Herzog documentary *Wings of Hope*. It's a short, obscure film about Juliane Koepcke, the sole survivor of an air crash in 1971. The passenger plane (carrying ninety-two people) she was on exploded after being struck by lightning and went down in the rainforest. The German title of the film is *Julianes Sturz in den Dschungel* (Juliane's Fall into the Jungle). Koepcke endured for some time alone, before walking for ten days through the dense bush to safety. Herzog, who was scouting locations for *Aguirre, the Wrath of God* at the time, was meant to be on the same plane. His reservation was cancelled at the last minute.

In the documentary, Herzog and Koepcke retrace her steps. They take the same flight, sit in the same seats and eventually return to the crash site. Given almost thirty years have elapsed since the accident, it is startling when they find sections of the plane still scattered among the trees. Parts of the fuselage are overgrown, covered in vines as if embraced by the jungle. Memory and place. A reminder that we are only passing through and that everything is part of something larger.

'Monotreme' exists because it almost happened. Many moons ago, I found myself travelling through Queensland with two Dutch backpackers. I was broke and they only picked me up so I could drive while they slept. We got along fine for a while and then they abruptly decided to dump me at a campsite in Eungella National Park, an hour west of Mackay. It was the off-season and, after they left, I was the only person there for a couple of days. Eventually, a kindly couple turned up, took pity on me and gave me a lift to

Mackay, where I caught a bus back to Brisbane (with a stowaway tick on my perineum, not that I knew it at the time).

While solo camping, I spent a lot of time sitting by Broken River, watching platypuses and their puggles. They didn't seem to mind I was there. I fantasised about joining them and making art together. In retrospect it's just as well that couple turned up.

'Here Be Leviathans' was written immediately after I finished *Mammoth*. I felt like I'd given sabretooth tigers a hard time in the novel, while making wolves out to be heroic figures. Which is strange for me, as I'm a cat man. I'm owned by Ripley the Korat and Elektra the Bengal. *The Age* erroneously (and hilariously) reported them as my daughters in an article, which, to be fair, isn't far from the truth.

One of the subjects I talked about most while promoting *Mammoth* was synthetic biology and the resurrection of extinct species. Efforts to bring back mammoths are now well documented, so here's an update on what other species we can expect to see roaming the Earth once more during our lifetimes: Chinese river dolphins, Glyptodonts (giant armadillos), dodo, thylacine, ground sloth (six metres long and weighing five tonnes) and the star of this story, *Smilodon*. Slightly more dangerous than Barbra Streisand's twin Coton de Tulear puppies, Miss Violet and Miss Scarlett, who are clones of her former companion Samantha, who died in 2017. Babs isn't the only one up to some major defiance of nature. Diane von Furstenberg had her Jack Russell terrier Shannon copied in 2016. The clone puppies are called Deena and Evita.

The thing is, as long as you can collect viable DNA and have deep pockets, you can clone pretty much anything now. It's not much of a leap to imagine a park like the one in this story, or that it will all go badly wrong. Thankfully we may never achieve a *Jurassic Park* scenario. Fossilised dinosaurs are too old.

In what has been an unexpected shift in my life, I was hired on the strength of *Mammoth* as an editor by Museums Victoria in 2021. One of my first tasks was to create a voice and personality for Horridus, the sixty-seven-million-year-old *Triceratops* specimen now on display at Melbourne Museum. I've also written two picture books for kids, *Horridus and the Hidden Valley* and *Horridus and the Night Forest* (illustrated by fellow Belfast boy Aaron Cushley), and edited the coffee-table book that accompanies the exhibition, *Horridus: Journey of a Triceratops.* I saw none of this coming when I was writing *Mammoth* and the title story in this collection. Now I'm mates with palaeontologists who dig up *Smilodon* and tyrannosaurs. Mind officially blown.

'The Strait of Magellan' is my attempt at an Edgar Allan Poe–style seafaring horror story, in the vein of *The Narrative of Arthur Gordon Pym of Nantucket*, and is a bitter pill for me. You likely rolled your eyes when you realised it was a viral pandemic story and, fair enough, we're all sick of that but, in my defence, I've been working on this for six years. It began when my mum, Liz, was diagnosed with early onset Alzheimer's. My sister, Julie, is a nursing home manager (whose life these past few years has been one of hellish torment) and she informed me in no uncertain terms of the realities our mum, and many of the residents under my sister's care, faced in living with Alzheimer's. Along with the terrifying loss of memories and gradual erasure of personality would come daily physical indignities and humiliations. We worried Liz might wind up like her mother, Ada, who had no clue who she or anyone else was during her final years, before bleeding out through her orifices while suffering a series of strokes and complete system collapse. My grandmother – who had one eye, was a former terrorist, and was tougher than you, me and everyone we know put together – died hard. At the end she screamed blue murder and then went quiet because she could see her mother. Her last words were, 'Mummy, is that you?'

Alzheimer's is brutal because it takes years for the sufferer to die. My sister used to say she wished it would happen quicker and that got me thinking. Then I read about amyloidosis in Antarctic, Californian and Australian sea-lion populations – a hardening of kidney tissue linked to urogenital carcinomas developing as a result of herpes. Sea lions bump into a rock and the brittle part of the kidney breaks off, causing massive internal haemorrhage and death. At the animal shelter, we took care of a batch of cats with amyloidosis. They were lovely animals, gentle and friendly, who'd been through the wringer in an illegal breeding facility. They lived with us at the shelter for a long time while their case stalled in the courts. Several didn't make it. They would jump down from a scratching post and, just like those sea lions, the kidney would fracture and they'd be dead within the hour.

In case you're freaking out right now, HHSV1-ABAD is an invention of mine. It doesn't exist. Though, as we know from COVID-19, we wouldn't last long if something bad did come down the pipeline.

My father, Ernie, my mum's carer despite his own multitude

of health issues, bounced in and out of hospital throughout 2020. Pneumonia, chest infections, crippling arthritis – you name it. He was another tough nugget. Ernie was a body builder and a truck driver. He smoked an elaborate pipe and refused to entertain a hearing aid, which meant the TV volume was always deafening. In February 2021, he was admitted to hospital yet again. This time, despite being double vaccinated with Pfizer, he contracted COVID-19 from a healthcare worker. He passed away a week later, on 16 February 2021. Due to international travel restrictions, I was unable to secure permission to leave Australia for the funeral. The old man maintained his macabre sense of humour to the bitter end. Turns out he chose a plot in the Antrim Cemetery next to the toilet block, for mourner convenience. Very thoughtful.

Unable to care for herself in his absence, Liz had to go into a nursing home. Julie knew a good one close to her place (not the one she manages – that would be too much). She's there now. She's happy. She has friends. She's eating well, for the first time in decades. She asks who the 'wee man' is in photos of Ernie, the husband she lived with for fifty-three years.

If you want to put a positive spin on this glum tale, think of Valeria Gómez sitting in the helm of the *Nemesis* at the end and imagine a sixty-thousand-word draft of this story that might just exist somewhere in my files. A draft where Valeria makes it to Puerto Williams and realises she is immune to Abaddon, as is every woman whose mother had Alzheimer's. A draft where the remnants of the Chilean Navy send her to Antarctica in search of a Russian researcher who is working on finding a cure by studying herpes and amyloidosis in sea lions. Maybe that story is out there, beyond the cliffs of ice. Maybe you'll read it one day.

—

'Alas, Poor Yorick' is, out of all the stories in this collection, the least fictional. In the early 1950s, frantic attempts were being made by the United States to propel primates into space, in preparation for sending people. For some reason all the monkeys were called Albert, with Albert VI nicknamed Yorick because of their poor record at making it back from the void. On 20 September 1951, Yorick plus eleven mice slipped the bonds of Earth and survived the landing in the New Mexico desert, the first to do so. It took the recovery team two hours to reach the sealed capsule. Tragically, Yorick and two of the mice overheated and perished in the meantime.

I wanted to write this story for years but couldn't find the right voice and approach. Then I went up for my first flying lesson, taking off from Tooradin Airfield, not far from where I live. The instructor was a seventy-year-old seven-foot-tall ex–Brazilian air force pilot, who, right from the start, made me do everything. The plane was old school. Lots of the analogue dials had stickers pasted over them that read *Non-functional*. We tasted the fuel beforehand to check for water content. I had to prime the magnetos, open the choke and not only start the aircraft myself but taxi onto the runway and take off. Once aloft, I flew over my home on Phillip Island, then, at the behest of my suspiciously relaxed instructor, performed some basic aerobatics. Not quite a loop-the-loop, but not far off. I landed the bird into the wind.

After, I asked the instructor if it was normal to give a newbie such complete control of an aircraft. He laughed and said, 'Definitely not, but you were so calm and unemotional – I knew you'd be fine.' Riding home on my motorbike, I almost barfed in my helmet once my guts realised what I'd just done. Strange that

I felt nothing at the time. No nerves, no excitement. I was almost bored. And there, at my computer that night, was Yorick.

'Shot Down in Flames' is one of those stories inspired by the work of another writer, in this case Thea Astley. Way back in 2013, I was one of the judges for *Meanjin*'s Tournament of Books (short story edition). The remit was to pick the best Australian short story of all time. It was quite the death-battle. The final two stories were 'Today on Dr Phil' by Tom Cho versus 'Hunting the Wild Pineapple' by Thea Astley. Dredging up my judge's notes, I notice I refer to 'Hunting the Wild Pineapple' as, 'like Cheever on mescaline, equal parts irritating and amusing, revelatory and downbeat'. In my youthful enthusiasm, I go on to describe Astley as 'the progenitor, the chain-smoking, wise-cracking, jazz-loving four-time Miles Franklin–winning champion of linguistic manipulation whose style got on Helen Garner's nerves and who pushed the envelope of Australian literature when no-one else had the cojones to do so'.

Gushing a bit, but I was excited by her work. I had just read Astley's Miles Franklin winners *The Well-Dressed Explorer* (1962), *The Slow Natives* (1965), *The Acolyte* (1972) and *Drylands* (1999) and was working on my second novel, *The Glass Kingdom*, at the time, which was heavily influenced by Astley's energy and landscapes, and read by virtually no-one. Incidentally, all of Astley's Miles Franklin winners are out of print. That gets on my nerves big-time, especially when you consider the books of the other four-time winner, Tim Winton, are readily available.

The narration in *The Slow Natives* jumps abruptly between

characters, sometimes mid-sentence when they pass each other in the streets of Brisbane. Reading that changed my thinking on how a story can be told from multiple perspectives. In 1972 – the year I was born – Astley said, 'My main interest is the misfit. Not the spectacular outsider, but the seedy little non-grandiose non-fitter who lives in his own mini-hell.' That's a description of virtually every writer I know, myself included. In fact, given what we've all been through these past few years, I reckon that describes most of us. They don't make them like Astley anymore. She wrote what she wanted and didn't give a shit. Long live the Queen.

'A Beautiful and Unexpected Turn' came about after Adelaide Writers' Week unwittingly put me in the same hotel room five years apart. Former directors Laura Kroetsch and Jo Dyer are the guilty parties here. That is some festival. Every time I attend, something weird happens. The last time I went, I started talking to the room as if it were an old friend. It had seen me before. I began to think about everyone who had passed through that room in the interim, who had slept in that bed. And I checked under the mattress (and under the bed), as I always do, in case some gangster has stashed money there.

It got me wondering about how much place influences our lives. What happened on a certain spot before we got there, and what will happen after we're gone? This led to watching a lot of time-lapse videos, months of footage filmed from a single fixed point. I love the ending to *Lucy* (2014), where Scarlett Johansson's character cycles back through everything that happened in history from where she's sitting in Times Square. We see New York unmade before our eyes.

Also, hotel rooms are erotic locations and I wanted to write a sex-positive consenting love story for couples where, for once, something good happens. Unfashionable, I know.

'Kiss Tomorrow Goodbye' is the hardest story in this collection to read and the one with the least number of changes since it first appeared on my screen. I don't remember writing it. I must've been in a fugue state at the time. I showed it to Tony Birch back in 2015 and he told me that he thought it was brilliant but good luck finding a publisher. Fortunately, UQP have a longstanding reputation of taking risks, and of supporting short stories. Otherwise this story, and indeed this collection, would never have seen the light of day. Aviva, Felicity and I have, at various times, scratched our heads in puzzlement as to how this story exists, how it came out of my brain. I can't explain that part, but what I can tell you is that its origin is, unbelievably perhaps, grounded in reality.

In 2011, I went to Las Vegas, not to gamble or cavort, but to visit the Neon Boneyard for an article I was writing, which later appeared in *Griffith Review* and *Financial Review*. At that time, the yard was only accessible by appointment, and I had to arrange for a permit to take photographs. It's now open to the public. A hot, precarious pile of metal signs, belonging to casinos and restaurants long since demolished, were stacked haphazardly behind a wire fence at the edge of the Mojave Desert. The heat was unbearable but the stories behind the old neon signs were fascinating.

At the time, I was books editor at *The Big Issue*, and found myself eschewing the glitz and glamour of the strip in favour of chatting with the many homeless people living on its periphery. They shared stories of rotten luck, costly mistakes, mental illness and lack of official support. When I asked how they tolerated the heat, I was told in hushed tones that some lived in the elaborate maze of tunnels underneath the city.

There are hundreds of people down there, spread out across almost two hundred miles of tunnels. They contend with nests of black widow spiders, rats, flash floods, harassment from Metro (Las Vegas Metropolitan Police Department) and the occasional rumoured alligator. *Las Vegas CityLife* reporter Matthew O'Brien paints a vivid portrait of the existence eked out by Nevada's forgotten people in his 2007 book *Beneath the Neon: Life and death in the tunnels of Las Vegas.*

A cab driver showed me the incomplete and abandoned casino in which JKa and her crew squat. There were people living in there, to whom site security turned a blind eye. The whole city stank of desperation, of a place that was barely clinging on despite the billions of dollars being wasted under everyone's noses. Transience, time and memory again. It struck me as I stood by a storm drain under a highway that one day it would all be covered in sand.

As for the Banksy-esque Cagney, well, let's just say that in the distant recesses of youth I may have occasionally found myself clinging precariously to the roof of a building in a city on the far side of the world, working out what size I should make the letters in *Each Dawn I Die.*

There were stories that we liked, and some we didn't, that could've been in this collection but aren't. Stories of drownings and Grindr dates, of car crashes and shoplifting, of seedy motels and sentient motorcycles, unlikely fashion models and costume-shop sex. A Brexit allegory. A twenty-thousand-word tale of a nightmarish wedding where the bride fantasises about being a colonist on one of Jupiter's moons.

They didn't fit. They weren't right. Thematically incompatible. They needed more work, or less. Will you ever lay eyes on these tales, friend? Maybe, but don't hold your breath. Short stories are misleadingly named. They take ages.